Marjorie Dean, Post-Graduate

Josephine Chase

Alpha Editions

This edition published in 2022

ISBN : 9789356785847

Design and Setting By
Alpha Editions
www.alphaedis.com
Email - info@alphaedis.com

Contents

CHAPTER I.
ON THE SANDS

"It's too perfect a night to stay on shore, girls and boys. Let's go for a moonlight cruise in the Oriole!" Hal Macy sprang up from the white sands where he had been devotedly lounging at Marjorie Dean's feet and held out his hands to her.

"Oh, glorious!" Marjorie gaily accepted the proffered hands. She laughed, with the sheer pleasure of youth, as Hal swung her to her feet. "My, what a strong person you are, Hal Macy!" she lightly commented as she freed her hands from Hal's lingering clasp.

"Glad *you* think so," emphasized Hal. He could not help wishing Marjorie were not quite so matter-of-fact.

"*I* don't think so," promptly disagreed Danny Seabrooke. "Macy is a weakling; a mere muscleless infant compared to me."

"Oh, see here, Danny Seabrooke, you'll have to eat that. Think I'll stand for any such talk? Eat it now, or else prove it," challenged Hal.

"I can prove it," Danny waved confidently. "Just watch me lift Geraldine from the shifting sands."

"Yes, just watch him," drawled Lawrence Armitage. He took up a guitar, temporarily idle on the sands, and began to strum it lightly. His deep blue eyes rested mirthfully on Danny and Jerry.

"Wait a second," Danny elaborately braced his feet in the sand. "Now, ready! Heave, heave, ho!"

Jerry suddenly let go of his hands and dropped back on the beach. "No, thank you." She pretended displeasure. "I don't care for your wonderful assistance." She directed a scornful glance at her would-be helper.

"You did that on purpose," accused Danny. "You are a cruel, cruel girl. Suppose I had lost my balance and dug my nose into the sand?"

"Sorry you didn't," was the unfeeling reply.

"Squabbling again," Laurie reached out a helping hand to Jerry and drew her to her feet. Danny looked sadly on.

"Please forgive me and continue to regard me as your friend. That's all I ask of you," he pleaded with stony Jerry.

"You talk like a popular song," she criticized. She broke into smiles when he knelt on the sand before her and contritely offered her his hand.

"Was that a compliment?" Danny grinned hopefully.

"Why should I throw bouquets at you? Can you think of a reason?" Jerry asked him. "I can't think of one."

"Neither can I," Danny agreed, and the squabblers burst into laughter.

"Isn't the moon wonderful tonight?" Standing beside Hal on the wide strip of gleaming beach Marjorie worshipped the white night. "Leila recites an old Irish poem about moonlight that must have been written for this night. It goes like this:

"The magic of yon sailing moon

Lures my poor heartstrings out of me;

God's moonshine whitens the lagoon;

The earth's a silver mystery."

Hal listened. His mind was centered on Marjorie rather than on the quaint bit of verse she was reciting. In her white lingerie frock, her vividly beautiful face raised toward the pale glory of the drifting moon, her loveliness filled Hal's boyish heart with worship.

He would have liked to tell her that he thought her far more wonderful than either the silvery moon or the most exquisite bit of Irish verse that had ever been composed. Long friendship with Marjorie warned him against such an avowal. She was so different from most girls about compliments. She did not like to be told that she had done well, while she positively loathed being told she was beautiful. She had a clever way of politely ignoring a compliment, then immediately changing a subject from personal to impersonal which Hal considered maddening.

Since the first week in July when the Deans had arrived at Severn Beach, there to spend a part of the summer, Hal had been trying to decide whether or not he should allow another summer to pass without telling Marjorie of his love for her. On that memorable autumn evening of last year when Constance and Laurie had announced their early approaching marriage Hal had been dejectedly certain that Marjorie had nothing to give him save friendship. He had resolved then never to ask her to marry him unless he should come to believe that she had experienced a change of heart toward him.

Lately, since Marjorie had come to stay at Severn Beach, where the Macys usually spent the summers, Hal had been sorely tempted to break his proud resolution. Constance and Laurie had returned from their winter in Europe and were visiting Hal and Jerry at Cliff House, the apartment hotel in which the Macy family lived. Their perfect happiness made Hal wonder wistfully why it was that Marjorie could not love him even half so fondly as Constance loved Laurie. He had been Marjorie's faithful cavalier for the same number of years that Laurie had been Constance's. Now Laurie had won Connie for his wife, while he and Marjorie were still, as she had often said, "just good friends."

This disheartening thought now flashed through his brain for perhaps the hundredth time that week. The calm friendly glance he forced himself to bend on Marjorie as she finished quoting the verse bore no sign of his disquieting reflections.

"Bully for the Irish!" he exclaimed with deceiving heartiness.

"You're not a bit under the magic spell of the white moonshine," she rebuked with a laughing, upward glance at Hal.

"How do you know I'm not?" His tones were teasing, but into his eyes had leaped a sudden purposeful gleam which told a different story. "Moonlight affects different persons in different ways. Wait till we take to the launch. Then I'll turn moony and sing sentimental songs. I'll give you a fine imitation of a moonstruck nut. I wouldn't dare try it on shore. I might be run in for disturbing the peace."

"Run in for disturbing the peace?" inquired a horrified voice at Marjorie's elbow. Danny Seabrooke peered apprehensively around Marjorie at Hal. "Ah, I understand." He grew apologetic. "You weren't speaking of me. You meant your—well—er—" Danny drew down his freckled face very sorrowfully. "When did it happen, Macy?"

"It hasn't happened yet, but it will soon," Hal promised with cool significance.

"I shan't be here to see it. I'm going to take a walk up the beach with Geraldine." Danny hastily fell behind a few steps and took Jerry by a plump arm. "Come along," he urged. "It's not safe around here."

"It's safe enough for me." Jerry briskly shook off Danny's detaining hand. "I'm going out in the Oriole. Hurry up, you sentimental strollers," she called over one shoulder to Constance and Laurie. They had paused for a moment, hand in hand, and were raptly gazing out to sea. "Come out of lovers' lane and join the crowd."

"Have a little more regard for our married dignity, Jeremiah," Laurie reminded. "Kindly remember that Connie and I came down to the beach this evening solely to look after you four children."

"Much obliged, but Dan-yell is the only one who needs a guardian of this illustrious bunch." Jerry bowed ironical thanks.

"All right for you, Jurry-miar Macy. I tried to be pleasant with you. I respectfully called you Geraldine. But no more!" Danny shook a displeased finger at Jerry. "I'm going to walk beside Constance."

"Poor Connie," groaned Jerry.

"Fortunate Connie, you mean," corrected Danny with a vast smile. "Do talk to me, Constance. Forget your husband for five seconds. You look so sympathetic. But you're not." Danny fixed an accusing glance on laughing Constance. "You're laughing at me."

"Why shouldn't I laugh at you, Danny Seabrooke? You're so funny and foolish."

"Funny and foolish." Danny cocked his head on one side and considered. "Nope, that's not sympathy. I'll have to try again. Let me see. Marjorie might appreciate me."

With a forward dive he caught Marjorie by one arm and began walking her rapidly up the beach and away from Hal. "Good-night, Mr. Macy," he flung back over one shoulder.

"Not yet," Hal cleared the widening space between him and Danny almost at a leap. "Now Dan-yell!" He grabbed Danny by the shoulders; spun him round until he faced down the beach. A vigorous push from Hal's avenging arms sent Danny careering down the beach at a mad gallop.

"Never touched me!" he sent back defiantly to Hal. He gave an agile sideways bounce, barely managing to dodge Jerry, Laurie and Constance in his headlong flight. "Good-bye. I'm never coming back!" he yelled at the trio.

Within the next three minutes Danny had changed his mind. "Fine night for a run," was his bland venture as he caught up with the three strollers. "Only I'd rather know beforehand that I was going to take a run. Macy is what I should call dangerous. He ought to be caged."

"Neither Jerry nor Danny will ever grow up," was Marjorie's amused remark as Hal returned to her side.

"I don't think you've grown up much, Marjorie," Hal burst forth with sudden eager wistfulness. "You look just as you did the first time I ever saw you; only you are even prettier than you were then."

Hal's stubborn restraint gave way before the uncontrollable impulse to speak his mind to Marjorie. "You were coming out the gate of Sanford High, and I wondered who you were," Hal went on boyishly. "I described you to

Jerry afterward, and asked all about you. She didn't know you very well then. I made her promise and double promise that she'd never tell you I quizzed her about you."

"And she never did," Marjorie gaily assured. "I never even suspected you two of having had a secret understanding about just me. Jerry is a good secret keeper. I'm glad college hasn't made me staid and serious. I've loved the good times I've had at Hamilton as much as I've loved the work. Now I'm ready to put my whole heart into work there so as to try to make Hamilton mean as much to other students as it has meant to me."

Marjorie had purposely hurried away from Hal's very personal admission. He now brought her back to it with an earnest abruptness which raised a brighter color in her face.

"I wish you'd stay in Sanford and make the old town seem as much to me as it used to," he said. "I have a standing grudge against Hamilton College. Can't help having one, even though you and Jerry do think it's the only place on the map."

"It's the only place on the map for us until our work is done, Hal," she defended. "Once I thought I couldn't leave General and Captain to go back to Hamilton next fall. I found I was hard-hearted enough to do even that for the sake of my work there. I'm having a gorgeous time at the beach! Still I'm almost impatient for next week to come and bring with it my mid-summer trip to Hamilton. You can understand, I'm sure, Hal, how I feel about the building of the dormitory."

"Work can't fill your life, Marjorie," Hal answered with a tender, unconscious deepening of tone. "See how happy Connie and Laurie are! They *love* each other. *That's* the real meaning of life. Not even music could come between them and love. Could anything be more perfect than their romance? I've wished always that it would be so with you and me. I've wanted to tell you this for a long time, but I——"

"I hate to complain of your sister, Macy, but it's necessary." Danny Seabrooke bounced into the midst of Hal's declaration of love.

"I'll disown you as my brother if you listen to what he says," Jerry appeared at Danny's elbow.

"Oh, go away off the beach, both of you!" Hal waved the contesting pair away from him. He wished both Danny and Jerry anywhere but close at hand.

"Shan't go a step," defied Jerry. "Never think, Hal Macy, that you can chase me into the Atlantic Ocean. *You* may walk with Dan-yell, I've had enough of him. Go ahead and untie the Oriole. I'm going to monopolize Marvelous Marjorie for a while." Jerry tucked an arm in one of Marjorie's.

"Only for about five minutes," stipulated Hal. He cast a half smiling, half challenging glance at Marjorie. "I want to talk to her myself. Come along, old Seabean," he motioned Danny.

The two young men ran ahead to untie the motor boat belonging to Hal which was tied up at the Cliff House pier. Marjorie drew a soft little breath of relief. Hal's significant rush of words had taken her unawares. Until now she had never failed to steer him away from anything approaching sentiment. Tonight, however, she had sensed a certain determined quality in his voice which was not to be denied. Hal did not intend to be kept from saying his say much longer.

CHAPTER II.
MUSIC AND MOONLIGHT

"I hear your voice across the years of waiting;

Out of the past it softly calls to me:

True love knows neither ebbing nor abating;

How long, dear heart, must we two parted be?"

sang Constance, a lingering, old-world sadness in her pure perfect tones. For a moment after the last note died out on the white balmy night no one spoke. Only the steady, even purr of the Oriole's engine broke the potent stillness which had fallen upon the sextette of young folks.

"That was a very sad song, Mrs. Lawrence Constance Armitage," complained Danny with a subdued gurgle. "It almost made we weep, but not quite. I happened to recall in time that I wasn't in the same class with dear heart; that I had never been parted from dear heart, or any other old dear. That put a smother on my weeps."

"Glad something did." Laurie had accompanied Constance's song on the guitar. He now sat playing over softly the last few plaintive measures of the song.

"It's a beautiful song, Connie," Marjorie said with the true appreciation of the music lover. "I love those last four lines, even if they are awfully hopeless. I never heard you sing it before. What is it called?"

"'*Sehnsucht.*' That means in German 'longing.' I found it last winter in a collection of old German love songs. I liked it so much that I tried to put the words into English. It's the only time I ever attempted to write verse. It turned out better than I had expected." There was a tiny touch of pride in the answer.

"Connie used to sing it often for an encore last winter. Then she always had to sing it again. People never seemed to get enough of that particular song." Laurie's voice expressed his own adoring pride in Constance.

"I don't wonder. The music is the throbbing, I-can't-live-without-you kind, same as the words. It gets even me. You all know how sentimental I am—not," Jerry declared.

"Why, may I ask, does it get you?" briskly began Danny. "Why——"

"You may ask, but that's all the good it will do you," Jerry retorted with finality. "Let me take the wheel awhile, Hal. You may sing a little for the gang.

I may not admire some points about you, but I'll say you can sing, even if you are my brother."

"Oh, let me sing," begged Danny. "You never heard me at my best."

"I hope I never shall." Jerry did not even trouble to glance at the modest aspirant for vocal glory. "Don't speak to me, if you can help it. Just hearing you speak might get on my nerves and make me fall overboard." She rose carefully in her seat in order to change places with Hal.

Hal had taken no part in the discussion which had followed Constance's song. He was leaning over the wheel, his clean-cut features almost sternly set as he sent the Oriole speeding through a gently rippling sea. His thoughts were moodily centered on Marjorie. Danny's and Jerry's untimely interruption upon his impulsive declaration of love was in the nature of a misfortune to him. His first feeling of vexation in the matter had deepened into one of dejection as he listened to Connie's song. He could not help wondering darkly if that was the way it would be with him. Would it become his lot to long some day for Marjorie, and vainly, across the years? He was sure of his love for her. He was sure it would never ebb nor abate. What about her love for him? Hal had nothing but doubts.

Last fall he had reluctantly come to the conclusion that Marjorie did not care in the least for him, other than in the way of friendship. It was only since she had come to Severn Beach that he had begun to take heart again. He had been her devoted companion, as of old, on all of the pleasure sails, drives and jaunts which the sextette of Sanford young folks had enjoyed. It had sometimes seemed to Hal that Marjorie was a trifle more gracious to him than of yore. He felt that she was fond of him in a comradely way. He could not recall an occasion since he had known Marjorie when she had accepted the attentions of another Sanford boy. That was one thing he might be glad of.

The white glory of the night, the tender beauty of the girl he adored, her avowed enthusiastic preference for work above all else in life had crystallized Hal's troubled resolve to ask Marjorie the momentous question which, somehow, he had never before found the right opportunity for asking. And Jerry and Danny had "butted in" and spoiled it! This was his rueful reflection as he silently allowed Jerry to replace him at the wheel.

"I won't be stingy with the wheel," he soberly assured his sister, "but you'd better ask Dan-yell to sing."

"Never. I have too much consideration for the rest of the gang," Jerry retorted.

"And I have myself to consider," flung back Danny. "I wouldn't sing if Jerry-miar dropped to her knees on the sand and begged me to. Understand, every one of you, I can sing, warble, carol, chant or trill. There is no limit to my vocal powers. There was a time when I might possibly have been persuaded to sing. That time is past."

"Thank you, Jerry," Laurie said very solemnly.

"You're welcome," chuckled Jerry. "Glad I could be so useful."

"O, don't be too ready to laugh. I may sing just for spite," Danny warned. "To sing, or not to sing? That is the question."

"Take time to think it over, Danny," laughed Marjorie. "While you are thinking Connie will sing the song of Brahms I like so much. Please, Connie, sing 'The Summer Fields,'" she urged. "Then you'll sing, won't you, Hal?" She turned coaxingly to Hal who had seated himself beside her on one of the built-in benches of the motor boat.

"Maybe," Hal made half reluctant promise. He was wishing he dared take Marjorie's slim hands, lying tranquilly in her lap, and imprison them in his own.

Glancing frankly up at him Marjorie glimpsed in his eyes a bright intent look which hardly pleased her. It was an expression which was quite new to his face. She thought, or rather, feared she understood its meaning. "He'll go on with what he started to say to me the very first chance he has," was her dismayed reflection. "Oh, dear; I wish he wouldn't."

Laurie had already begun a soft prelude to "The Summer Fields." Marjorie had immediately looked away from Hal and out on the moonlit sea. She had the impression that Hal's eyes were still upon her. She felt the hot blood rise afresh to her cheeks. For a brief instant she was visited by a flash of resentment. Why, oh, why, must Hal spoil their long, sincere friendship by trying to turn it into a love affair?

Again Constance's golden tones rose and fell, adding to the enchantment of the night. Marjorie's instant of resentment took swift wing as she listened to the wistful German words for which the great composer had found such a perfect setting. She was glad she loved music and moonlight and poetry and all the beautiful bits of life. She did not wish life to mean the kind of romance Hal meant. Her idea of romance meant the glory of work and the stir of noble deeds.

"Now it's your turn, Hal. It's not fair to make me do all the singing. Jerry claims she can't sing, and she won't let Danny sing. Laurie makes me do his share of it. Marjorie can sing, but she thinks she can't. That leaves only you, and you haven't a ghost of an excuse. Go ahead now. Be nice and sing the Boat Song." Constance ended coaxingly.

"All right, Connie. Instruct your husband to play a few bars of it strictly in tune and I'll see what I can do." Hal straightened up suddenly on the bench with an air of pretended importance.

"See to it that your singing's strictly in tune," Laurie advised. "I can be trusted to do the rest." Already his musician's fingers were finding the rhythmic introduction to Tosti's "Boat Song."

"The night wind sighs,

Our vessel flies,

Across the dark lagoon."

Hal took up the swinging measures of the song in his clear, sweet tenor and sent it ringing across the water. Tonight he came into a new and sombre understanding of the song. Never before had he realized the undercurrent of doubt it contained. Perhaps Tosti had composed the song out of his own lover's hopes and fears. Unconsciously Hal's weight of troubled doubt went into an impassioned rendering.

Laurie and Constance understood perfectly his unintentional betrayal of his feelings. Danny, razor keen of perception, also grasped the situation. This time he had nothing to say.

"And here am I,

To live or die;

As you prove hard or kind;

Prove hard or kind."

Jerry sat looking unduly solemn as Hal tunefully voiced the sentimental, worshipping lines and took up the echoing refrain. When the song ended an odd silence fell which no one of them seemed willing to shatter. Connie and Laurie were frankly holding hands, their young faces touched with a romance born of music and moonlight. Danny was staring intently at Jerry as though absorbed in her management of the wheel.

Marjorie sat bathed in moonlight, looking unutterably lovely and trying her utmost not to appear self-conscious. She was under the blind impression that she alone understood what lay behind Hal's song. In reality she understood less concerning the strength of his love and devotion for her than did those who had been their intimate girl and boyhood friends. She did, however, detect a certain melancholy tinge to his singing which gave her a peculiar conscience-stricken feeling.

"No, I don't care to sing any more tonight," he said, when Laurie came out of his dream and asked him to sing an old Spanish serenade. "I'm not in a singing humor."

"Poor old Hal," Jerry was thinking as she gave the wheel an impatient turn by way of showing her disapproval. "He does love her so! Marjorie's the sweetest girl ever, but she's hard, not kind, when it comes to love. She's a regular stony heart."

CHAPTER III.
"SOMETHING TO REPORT"

"Tomorrow? Let me think." Marjorie's dark brows drew thoughtfully together. "Why, I'm not going anywhere, Hal." Marjorie made an effort to be casual which was only half successful. "I'm going to be busy packing. I shall have to take an early train for Hamilton on Thursday morning so as not to reach there late at night. I won't have a minute's spare time Thursday morning. I'll have to be ready as ready can be on Wednesday night."

The boating party had left the Oriole once more tied to the pier and had strolled back along the sands to Cliff House. To her surprised relief, Hal had not attempted to renew the subject she dreaded to discuss. In fact he had had very little to say. Responsive to this new mood of his she had walked beside him almost in silence, smiling at the animated discussion Jerry and Danny kept up all the way to the hotel. Laurie and Connie were as mute as she and Hal. Such understanding silences were characteristic of them, however.

As ardently as he had courted an opportunity to tell Marjorie he loved her Hal now upbraided himself for having been so stupid as to blurt out his feelings "when the gang were around." He would finish telling her what he had begun to say when Danny and Jerry had interrupted. He was resolved on that point. He was also determined that she should hear him out before she left Severn Beach on her mid-summer trip to Hamilton.

"Can't you find time to go out in the Oriole with me tomorrow afternoon, Marjorie?" There lurked a trace of stubborn purpose in Hal's question. "It will be our last sea voyage in the good ship, Oriole, this summer, you know. I suppose you will go from Hamilton back to Sanford." Hal eyed her almost gloomily.

Marjorie nodded. The two had reached the main entrance of the hotel a trifle ahead of their chums. They now stood waiting at the foot of the wide, ornamental flight of steps which led up to the central veranda of the enormous white stone hotel.

"I'll try to go for a part of the afternoon, Hal," she promised, careful to keep reluctance out of her voice. Pinned down to answer directly she had not the stony-heartedness with which Jerry had ticketed her. She could not flatly refuse the invitation of her boy friend of long standing.

"Good work! Which part?" Hal instantly brightened. "Let us settle that point before you have time to change your mind and back out," he said boyishly.

"The very idea! You only say that, Hal Macy," Marjorie retorted with playful emphasis. "I'm not a mind changer, nor a backer-out, either."

"Beg your pardon, and double beg it." Hal allowed a teasing note to creep into the answer. Already he was feeling less dejected. He had been half afraid that Marjorie might refuse to go for a last ride in the Oriole.

The swift unbidden reflection that Marjorie might not be quite so indifferent to him as he had thought brought a sudden flush to his cheeks and an odd new sense of hope to his sore heart. She could hardly have failed to understand the import of what he had begun to tell her on the way to the boat. Yet she had not refused to go for a ride with him on the morrow. She must surely have guessed the hidden reason for his invitation to her.

"Say, what time, Marjorie," Hal again urged. "All afternoon would suit me best," he added boldly.

"You can't have all afternoon." Marjorie lightly objected. "I'll have to hurry like mad in order to squeeze the ride into tomorrow's program. I'll be ready to go as soon as luncheon's over. I must be back at my packing by not a minute later than three o'clock. You and Jerry had better come to our table for luncheon. Is Jerry going with us?" Marjorie made a last attempt to ward off what appeared to be inevitable.

"No, she isn't. I haven't asked her," was the pointed reply. "Thank you, but I won't be at the hotel until I come up for you. I'm going to Carver's Island early in the morning to see a crowd of fellows I know who have a bungalow there. You usually have luncheon at one, don't you? I'll meet you in the Dresden lounge at half past one. Then we won't lose any of your precious time," Hal concluded almost grimly.

"All right," Marjorie assented. She was glad Hal had used a mildly peremptory tone. She had always admired his courteous, but positive, manner of settling a matter.

"Why in such a hurry?" Laurie questioned indolently as he and Constance now mounted the steps. "You two walked ahead of us as though you were on a training hike. Is that the way to appreciate a heavenly night like this?"

"It is when it's after ten o'clock and one has to be up and doing by seven tomorrow morning," flung back Marjorie. "You forget, Mr. Laurie Armitage, that *I'm going away, day after tomorrow.*" She emphasized each word with a vigorous bob of the head.

"No; none of us have forgotten that, Marjorie," Laurie bent a sudden warm friendly smile on her.

"We're going to miss you dreadfully, Lieutenant." Constance put an arm around Marjorie. The two stood and swayed back and forth schoolgirl fashion.

"Not half so much as I shall," Hal voiced frank regret. "Marjorie is a real pal. I'm going to miss her at every turn and corner. I'm going to annex myself to the Armitage family and become a pest after Marjorie goes."

"Go as far as you like, old man," Laurie invited. "Connie and I will do our best to amuse and cherish you."

"Cherish! Ah-h-h!" gurgled Danny who had just come up with Jerry. "Such a sweet word! Did anybody ever hear Jurry-miar say it to me?" He rolled his eyes and clasped his hands. "Silence? What? Don't all speak at once. No? I thought not."

"No one ever *will* hear me say it to you," Jerry told him in a tired tone.

"How ought I to receive such a remark?" Danny eyed her dubiously. "Answer me, Jurry-miar." He leaned far forward and stared fixedly at Jerry.

Her stolid expression deserted her. She had to laugh at the ludicrous set of Danny's freckled features. "Oh, never mind," she conceded. "Let's be amiable to each other for ten minutes. I'll hold the stop watch."

"U-h-h-h!" Danny simulated collapse. "This is so unexpected. Hurry up, gang. Let's go to the palm grotto for ices. If we hustle, Jur—I mean, Geraldine and I can sit at the same table without snapping at each other. Come, boys," he beckoned grandly to Hal and Laurie. "Gentlemen will be treated to ices as well as ladies. Think of that!" He smirked patronizingly at the two young men.

"I oughtn't linger longer," gaily demurred Marjorie. "Truly, Danny, I——"

She went to the palm grotto, however, marched there between Hal and Danny. During the enjoyable half hour the young people spent over the ices Hal was his usual jolly, light-hearted self. Marjorie welcomed the change in him from sombre seriousness to his old care-free manner. When she left him with a friendly good night at the door of the Dean's apartment she could have almost believed him to be the Hal of her high school days, had not the memory of his earnest words flashed across her brain. She could still hear him saying: "I've wished always that it would be so with you and me," in the eager, impassioned fashion which awoke no responsive echo in her heart.

She stepped into the living room her usually bright face so pre-occupied that it at once caught Mrs. Dean's attention as she smilingly glanced up from the magazine she held.

"I won't qualify for the early bird class in the morning, I'm afraid," Marjorie said with the merest suspicion of a smile. "Never mind; I'm going to get up early even if I do lose some sleep."

"Was that what made you look so sober as you came in, Lieutenant?" Mrs. Dean asked, amused surprise in the question.

"Did I look very sober?" Marjorie quickly countered.

"*Very*," emphasized her mother.

"Well," Marjorie paused, "I felt sober. Where's General, Captain?" She glanced questioningly toward the next room.

"He and Mr. Macy motored down to Logan Beach this evening to see a game of chess between two expert players, both friends of Mr. Macy's. He'll hardly be home before midnight." Mrs. Dean continued affectionately to watch Marjorie.

"Oh-h-h." Marjorie dropped down on a low chair. For a moment she sat plaiting little folds in the soft white evening scarf, now fallen into careless disarrangement across one shoulder. "Oh," she said again. "Er-oh, dear! I've something to report, Captain. I wish I hadn't. I couldn't report it to General as I can to you. It's about Hal. He's going to ask me to marry him. I *wish* he *wouldn't*."

The vehemence with which Marjorie voiced the disquieting report brought a shadowy flash of concern to her mother's face. It faded instantly into a distinctly humorous expression.

"How do you know Hal is going to ask you to marry him?" she quizzed, her eyes twinkling. "You've heard the old sad tale of Miss Betty Baxter who refused Captain Jones before he axed her."

"Oh-h, Captain!" Marjorie made a laughing open-armed rush at her mother. "Stop making fun of me. My case isn't a bit like silly Miss Betty Baxter's. What an idiotic person she must have been! You see, dearest," she slid an arm about her mother's neck. "Why—Hal——" Her color mounted to her white forehead—"began to ask me down on the beach tonight. Then Danny and Jerry came up to us. *They* didn't know what he was saying to me, of course. He surprised me, too."

Hesitatingly, Marjorie went on to tell her captain of her talk with Hal on the beach which had led up to his impulsive declaration of love. It was not easy to repeat, even to her mother. She had taken a stand behind her mother's low-backed chair, arms dropped forward. One hand patted a light tattoo on her mother's shoulder as she talked. Presently her voice trailed off into silence. Her head went down against her mother's neck.

"Bring over the low stool, Lieutenant," Mrs. Dean ordered in her briskest "army" tone.

"Yes, Captain." Quick as a flash Marjorie's arms dropped from her captain's shoulders. She left a light kiss on her mother's soft brown hair, then marched across the room for the stool. She set it down at her captain's feet, saluted and stood at rigid attention.

"Break ranks. Discipline seems to be still alive in the army," Mrs. Dean observed with a smile.

"It is." Marjorie settled herself on the cushioned stool and leaned her elbows on her mother's knees. She looked up inquiringly, face between hands. "What is it, Captain? You haven't said *one* word of what you think about—about Hal and me."

"I'm thinking for a moment of what I had best say." Mrs. Dean looked fondly down at the lovely colorful face raised to her own.

For an instant neither spoke. Then Mrs. Dean said with kindly deliberation: "If you loved Hal in the same whole-hearted way in which I believe he loves you, General and I should be glad of your engagement to him. General thinks Hal a man among young men. You know how much that means. We have occasionally discussed your long friendship with Hal and his entire devotion to you. We know that you do not love him. We are sorry that you cannot return his great affection for you." One hand strayed caressingly over Marjorie's curls. There followed another brief interval, then: "We wish you to be true to yourself, Lieutenant. That is the order of the day."

"Dearest and best," Marjorie reached for her mother's hands, took them in her own and fondled them; "why, oh, why didn't I fall in love with Hal as Connie did with Laurie? I don't know why. I'll have to tell him so tomorrow and it will hurt me almost as much to say it as it will hurt him to hear it. He's been such a splendid comfy friend. I can't bear to say 'no' to him, and I can't say 'yes.' It's a hard detail, Captain, but I must face it as a true soldier should. All I can do is tell Hal frankly, but in the best way I can, that I don't love him and never shall."

CHAPTER IV.
I CAN'T GIVE YOU UP, DEAR

"Let me conduct your marvelous majesty to a seat beside the wheel." Hal offered his hands with a motion of exaggerated gallantry. He caught Marjorie's hands in his own and half swung her down from the little pier and into the motor boat.

"Thank you, gallant and distinguished skipper," was Marjorie's blithe response as she sat down on the small cushioned bench nearest the wheel, guided by Hal's devoted arm.

"I had no idea you appreciated me so highly." He managed to keep up the light, bantering tone he had first used. It was not easy. What he longed to say to her as she turned her vivid, sparkling face toward him was: "I love you. I love you."

"Why shouldn't I appreciate you?" Marjorie merrily insisted. She was relieved at Hal's apparently light mood. She hoped it would continue for at least the greater part of the ride. She preferred to ward off the dreaded talk as long as she could. She had agreed with her captain that Hal had the right to be heard; that it was not fair to him to evade longer an understanding with him.

"I don't know. Why should you?" countered Hal.

"For two splendid reasons. You're taking me for a ride in the Oriole. Besides, you called me 'marvelous majesty,' which is a most flattering title. Oh, Hal Macy!" Marjorie exclaimed with animated irrelevancy; "isn't this the most heavenly blue and white and gold day? Blue sea, blue sky, white clouds and golden sun!"

"It's a peach of a day," he tersely agreed. Marjorie's declared appreciation of himself brought a half ironical smile to his lips. As usual, it was like that of a child, grateful for benefits. "What port?" he inquired briefly of her as he started the Oriole away from the pier.

"No port," was Marjorie's prompt choice; "just a little run out to sea."

"Right-o." Hal obediently headed the Oriole seaward. "Look at the crowd!" He indicated with a sweep of an arm the flock of white-winged sail boats and motor launches which thickly dotted the dimpling water. "Every fellow at the beach who owns a boat seems to be out with it today."

"It's an ideal day for boating," Marjorie found herself tritely echoing Hal's opinion of the weather. Still she could not on the instant think of anything else to say. Her usual fund of gay, amusing conversation had deserted her. She was too honest of spirit to pretend that which she did not feel.

"There's no danger of a sudden squall, either." Hal's interest in the weather appeared to deepen. "This day is what I'd call an old reliable. Storms hardly ever blow up out of such honest-to-goodness blue skies as these."

"That's true." Marjorie inwardly derided herself for being such an utter stupid. She tried to make herself believe that it was only Hal, her boy chum, with whom she was out boating. She could not. The young man at the wheel whose familiar handsome features were touched with an intensity of purpose quite foreign to them was all but a stranger to her. In the past she had had only rare, disquieting glimpses of the intense side Hal was showing today.

A flat, uncomfortable silence suddenly drifted down upon them. Hal's courteous attempt to talk trivialities, simple because he knew that was what Marjorie preferred him to do was a failure. He had come to the place where he could no longer continue to hide his heart from her.

The silence between them continued; deepened. Both had begun to feel the tensity of the situation. Both had tried to talk pleasantries and both had failed. Hal occupied himself with sending the Oriole scudding cleverly in and out among the numerous pleasure craft, large and small which dotted the course he was steadily taking toward quieter more aloof waters.

Now and again they were briskly hailed by the occupants of other passing boats. Hal lightened momentarily as he answered the merry salutations, then relapsed into somber gravity.

"What a lot of people you know at Severn Beach, Hal." Marjorie was glad to find her voice again. Hal was waving an acknowledgment to a noisy, rollicking crew of young men in a passing power launch who had sent out a ringing hail to him.

"I only know a bunch of yachtsmen and a few other fellows." Hal disclaimed popularity with a shrug of his broad shoulders. "The Clipper, my racing sailboat, is better known along this coast than I am. Oh, but she's a winner!" Hal brightened with pride of ownership. "She won every race I entered her for last summer. She's won two this season, and she's entered in a spiffy race the yacht club is going to pull off in a couple of weeks. You'd better stay at the beach and see it. I'll take you aboard for the race, if you'll stay." Half laughingly, half pleadingly he offered this bribe.

"That would be glorious; to be in a real race!" Marjorie looked her regret. "You're always so good to me, Hal; always planning some perfectly dandy stunt just to please me. But you know how it is about Hamilton. I feel it truly a sacred obligation; my work there, I mean. I couldn't allow personal pleasure to come before it."

"No; nor love, either," Hal burst forth with a hurt vehemence which brought the hot blood to Marjorie's cheeks. "I beg your pardon, Marjorie," he said almost immediately afterward. "I spoke on impulse. Still, that's the way I feel about your going back to Hamilton next fall when I love you so dearly and want you to marry me. I wish you cared even half as much for me as you do for your work at Hamilton. But you don't care at all."

"I do care for you, Hal, as one of the best friends I have," Marjorie protested, raising her brown eyes sorrowfully to Hal's clouded face.

"I know," Hal rejoined a shade less forcefully. "I value your friendship, Marjorie, more highly than I can say. But friendship's not what I want from you, dear girl. I love you, truly and forever. I've loved you since first you came to Sanford to live. I'd have told you so long ago but you never gave me an opportunity." Hal paused. He regarded Marjorie wistfully; questioningly.

"I—I know it, Hal," she admitted reluctantly, but with her usual honesty. "I—I haven't wished you to talk of love to me. There were times last winter"—she stopped in confusion—"when I thought you cared—a little. I—I wasn't sure."

"Be very sure of it, now." Hal's reply was a mixture of tenderness and dejection.

"I don't want you to love me, Hal," Marjorie cried out almost sharply in her desire to be emphatic. "Last night, after what you said to me on the beach, I couldn't help but be sure. I—I told Captain of it. I always tell her everything. Captain is sorry I don't love you. She and General are fond of you. They'd be happy if we were—if we were—to become engaged." Marjorie spoke the last words hesitatingly.

"I'm glad you told your mother. You know how fine I think both General and Captain are." Hal fought back the hurt look that threatened to invade his face. He gripped the wheel until his knuckles stood out whitely against the sun-tanned brown of his hands.

Marjorie caught a glimpse of the unhappiness which sprang straight from her old comrade's sore heart and into his eyes.

"There; I've hurt you, Hal! Truly I never meant to!" she exclaimed in quick contrition.

"Never mind me." Hal made a gesture of self-depreciation. "It isn't your fault because you can't find it in your heart to love me." He forced a smile, proudly trying to conceal his own desolation of spirit.

Her eyes remorsefully fixed on him the smile did not deceive Marjorie. Hal's tensity of feature informed her of the weight of the blow she had just dealt him.

"Please, please, Hal, forgive me!" she begged with a sudden excess of pained humility.

"Forgive you? For what?" Hal bent a fond questioning glance on Marjorie's troubled face.

"For—for—not loving you," she faltered. "It hurts me dreadfully to know that I must be the one to make you unhappy. Forgive me for seeming to be so hard and unsympathetic about love. I've never thought of it for myself. It has always seemed vague and far away; like something not a part of my life. I know the love between Connie and Laurie is wonderful. I can appreciate their devotion to each other. I have the greatest impersonal reverence for love and lovers. But for me life means endeavor and the glory of achievement."

The voice of ambitious, inspirited youth sang in her tones, half appealing though they were. Came an embarrassed stillness between them. Hal's face, strong, even stern in its self-repression was turned partly away from her. The bleakness of his suffering young soul peered forth from his deep blue eyes as he stared steadily across the dimpling sun-touched waves.

"Nothing matters in life but love. To love and to be loved in return," he said slowly, but with a kind of fatalistic decision. "You'll love someone, someday, even though you can't love me." The shadow on Marjorie's face deepened as she listened. It was almost as though in a flash of second sight Hal were telling her a fortune she did not care to hear. "When love truly comes to you, then you'll understand what you can't understand now," he ended.

"I don't want love to come to me. I don't wish to understand it," Marjorie made sad protest. "Since it isn't in my heart to love you, I should never wish to love any one else. You're the finest, gentlest, truest boy *I've* ever known, Hal, or ever expect to know."

Hal's half averted face was suddenly turned toward Marjorie. Across it flashed a rare sweet smile which lived long afterward in her memory. "It's as I told you last night, Marjorie Dean. You haven't grown up." Tender amusement had mercifully broken into and lightened his gloom. "You only think you have," he said. Marjorie's naive avowal had brought with it a faint stirring of new hope.

"Yes, Hal, I've grown up," Marjorie began seriously. "It's not——"

"You'll never really grow up until love finds the way to your heart," Hal interrupted with gentle positiveness. "I hope when it does it will be love for me. I can't give you up, dear. I'm going to call you 'dear' this once. I'd rather have your friendship than the love of any other girl in the world. I'm going to wait for you to grow up."

CHAPTER V.
A WARM RECEPTION

"Hamilton! Hamilton!" Marjorie Dean smiled to herself. Her expressive brown eyes grew brighter as the lusty call echoed through the car. One hand tightened about the leather handle of her traveling bag with the impatience of one who was longing to be free of the limited confines of the car. She peered alertly out of the open window at the familiar railway platform which lay deserted in the warm glory of a mid-summer sun. How strange it seemed to see the good old platform so bare and empty!

"Not a sign of Robin," was her disappointed reflection. "What's happened to her, I wonder? I'm evidently first here after all. She can't have arrived yet or she would surely be out on the platform watching for me."

The three or four persons, whose destination was also Hamilton were now moving down the aisle toward the car's upper door. Marjorie did not follow the orderly little line of passengers. She turned and hurried to the opposite end of the car impatient to be out of the train. She was glad to be the only one to leave the car from that end.

"Oh-h-h." She drew a half sighing breath of sheer loneliness. "What a dismal old place!"

She ran lightly down the car steps, eluding the brakeman's helping hand, and came to an abrupt stop on the deserted platform. She stood still, casting a faintly disconsolate glance about her. It was hard, indeed, to believe that this empty space with the warm friendly sunshine streaming down upon it was Hamilton station, endeared to her by the memory of many happy meetings and cheerful goodbyes on the part of student friends.

"What had I better do?" was her next thought. "What a goose I was not to tear Jeremiah from the beach and bring her with me. Robin's missing from the picture. That means I'll have to be on the watch for her. How I'd like to walk in on Miss Remson at Wayland Hall this afternoon! Wouldn't she be surprised, though?"

Marjorie cast a meditative glance toward the staid drowsy town of Hamilton. Robina Page, her classmate and partner of the good little firm of "Page and Dean," as their chums liked to call them, had written that she would meet Marjorie at the station. From her handbag Marjorie extracted Robin's latest letter to her. She glanced it over hurriedly. Yes; it read: "Friday afternoon, July 25th. I'll be at the station to meet the three-twenty train. Don't dare disappoint me."

"It looks as though I'd be the one to meet the trains," she murmured under her breath. Always quick to decide she made the choice between waiting patiently in the station building for the next train Robin could arrive on, or seeking the grateful coolness of the Ivy, in favor of the dainty tea shop. The train Robin might be on would not arrive until five-thirty.

Picking up her traveling bag which she had momentarily deposited on the platform Marjorie moved briskly toward the flight of worn stone steps leading to the station yard.

"If Robin shouldn't be on the five-thirty train I suppose I'd best go to the Congress Hotel and stay there until tomorrow. If I should go on to the campus alone, I'd miss seeing her; that is, if she should arrive tonight. I'll fairly absorb time tables and meet all the trains tonight except the very late ones," was Marjorie's energetic resolve as she swung buoyantly along the smooth wide stone walk. The brief moment of depression which she had felt at sight of the empty station platform had now vanished. She was again her sunny self, animated and bubbling over with the desire for action.

She was so intent upon her own affairs she quite failed to see three laughing faces frame themselves suddenly in a screened window of the station. Almost instantaneous with their appearance they were withdrawn. Their owners made a noiseless, speedy exit from the waiting room and flitted through the open doorway which led to a square of green lawn behind the building bounded by cinder drives.

Giggling softly as they ran the stealthy trio gathered in a compact little group at a rear corner of the building which Marjorie must pass on her way across the yard to the street.

"I'll relieve you of that bag, lady," croaked a harsh, menacing voice. The bag was snatched from Marjorie's hand in a twinkling.

"Hands up!" ordered a second voice, only a shade less menacing than that of the first bandit.

"Boo, boo-oo, woo-oo-oo!" roared a third outlaw. The final "oo" ended in a sound suspiciously like a chuckle.

Completely surrounded by an apparently merciless and lawless three Marjorie had not attempted to retrieve the traveling bag. Instead she had pounced upon the smallest of the bandits with a gurgle of surprised delight.

"Vera Mason, you perfect darling! Where did you come from, Midget, dear?" Marjorie laughingly quoted as she warmly kissed tiny Vera.

"Out of the everywhere into the here," Vera carelessly waved an indefinite hand and smiled up at Marjorie in her charming, warm-hearted fashion.

"And you, Leila Greatheart! So you've turned highwayman! I am pretty sure that I am the first victim. Very likely you planned with your partners in crime to practice on me. Give me my bag, you old villain." Marjorie shook a playful fist at Leila.

The widely smiling Irish girl merely reached out her strong arms, gleaming whitely against her dark blue gown, and gathered Marjorie into them. She kissed her on both cheeks, then placed a finger under Marjorie's chin and gazed admiringly at her.

"Beauty is Beauty, at home or abroad," she declared lightly. "And it's myself that has longed for a sight of you, little, beautiful lieutenant."

"Don't monopolize the victim," protested an aggrieved voice. Robin Page now made an attempt to pry Marjorie free from Leila's close embrace.

"Robin Page, you wicked girl! So this is the way you meet me at the station!" Marjorie hugged and kissed Robin with fresh enthusiasm.

"You will kindly blame these two rascals here for the hold-up," laughed Robin. "This pair, Lawless Leila and Vera, the Midge, are quite capable of dark deeds. Aren't those names I made up for them dandy? I'm going to write a play this year, a real melodrama, and have them play the leads under those very names. That's an inspiration born of this hold-up," she added in her bright fashion.

"And to think I was ever sad a minute over you three blessed geese!" Marjorie looked from one to another of her chums, her eyes bright with affection. "I thought of you all as I was leaving the train and was so sorry that you were, as I supposed, so far away. And all the time you were hanging around a corner fairly aching to hold me up. Oh, I'm so glad to see you! I've been looking forward to seeing Robin, but I never dreamed such good fortune as this was in store for me."

"She means us." Vera gave Leila a significant nudge.

"She does that," Leila purposely lapsed into a brogue. "And it's something grand I'll be saying to her yet, but not till I know myself what I'm going to say."

"Oh, never mind the blarney. Just tell me how you happen to be here," begged Marjorie, tucking an arm into Robin's. "Not one letter have I had from either of you since the Dean family went down to Severn Beach, and only one apiece since college closed. I may not be a prompt correspondent, but——"

"Tell me nothing." Leila put up a defensive hand. She was laughing behind it. "Isn't it I who know my own failings?"

"You ought to know by this time that you are a flivver as a correspondent," Marjorie condemned with pretended severity. "I thought, when I did not hear from you, that you and Midget had really gone to Ireland for the summer. You know you talked of taking the trip last spring. I supposed——"

"I was busy pointing out the Blarney Stone to Midget and capturing banshees and leprechauns for her to play with," interposed Leila. "No, Beauty; not this summer. Truth is truth. We did talk about a visit to the Emerald Isle during the summer, but Commencement morning changed all that. Midget and I planned then to come to Hamilton instead and give you a mid-summer welcome. Why, Midget and I said to each other, should we go gallivanting about old Ireland when the good little firm of Page and Dean would be working their dear heads off at Hamilton?"

"Why, indeed?" echoed Vera. "We're here to stay as long as you and Robin stay."

"We've been at Wayland Hall for a week waiting for you two promoters to appear. We didn't know the exact date of your appearance, or which one of you would appear first," Leila informed Marjorie.

"You talk as though Robin and I were a couple of rare elusive comets," Marjorie joked.

"You're a couple of rare, elusive P. G.s whose present mission is to lighten and gladden Leila's and my declining years," retorted Vera. "That's the real reason you came to Hamilton this July, though you may not have suspected it. Of course, while you're here, and we're here, we won't object to your doing a few kindly little stunts for our Alma Mater." Vera endeavored to appear extremely condescending. Instead she looked so utterly happy that Marjorie wrapped her arms about the dainty little girl and embraced her all over again.

"I reached here just one train ahead of you, Marjorie," Robin now said. "I was held up, too, and forced into a conspiracy against you. It happened to be more convenient for me to take an earlier train. I intended to meet yours anyway—you know the rest." Robin gestured eloquently toward Leila and Vera.

"Yes, I know the rest," Marjorie repeated fondly. "I also know something else. I was bound for the Ivy when three footpads waylaid me. Just to show you what a forgiving spirit I have I will invite those three footpads to a feast at the Ivy. I've had nothing to eat since early this morning and I'm famished. There was no dining car on the train."

"Ah, let me be the Irish lady to give the feast," wheedled Leila. "My gold burns in my pocket when it's too long there. Midget has far more money than she ought to have. All week we have led a cat and dog life, grumbling and sputtering about which of us should treat."

"All right. You're so smooth. I can't resist you, this once. I hereby invite you all to dinner at Baretti's tonight," stipulated Marjorie. "I've gold of my own to spend. Just as General put me on the train this morning he put an envelope in my hand. I opened it after the train had started. In it were two fifty dollar notes and a funny short letter from him telling me to call the money the Marjorie Dean Entertainment Fund. He ordered me to spend it just for good times. I must obey my general, you know. When I come back to Hamilton next——"

A sudden jubilant clamor from her chums drowned her voice.

"Aha!" Leila paused in the middle of the walk and waved a triumphant arm. "What do I hear?"

"Uh-h-h; but that's good news!" Robin made a show of collapsing from sheer relief.

"Is it really settled. Marvelous Manager?" Vera cried with some anxiety.

"Now you may tell me, Beauty, what I said last June you would say." Leila was radiant at the good news.

Marjorie laughed. "You are a soothsayer, Leila Greatheart," she said, obeying Leila's joyful command. "Yes; it has all been settled." Her own features reflected the good cheer of her friends. "I'm coming back to the campus in the fall."

CHAPTER VI.
IN LOVE WITH WORK

"To the boldest bandit belongs the spoils." Leila lifted Marjorie's traveling bag from the walk, took hold of her arm and began steering her across the grassy station yard to where a smart grey car stood on the drive.

"I'll let you tug it along to punish you for being a desperado. It's a heavy old thing. Fifteen minutes ago I didn't know where it and I would stop for the night. Now, thank goodness, and you girls, we can all go to Wayland Hall." Marjorie smiled over her shoulder at Robin and Vera who were walking behind them.

"What a love of a car!" she exclaimed as they neared the trim gray roadster. "I'll make a guess. It's Vera's. Somehow it suggests her."

"Yes, it's Vera's. Have you noticed? My eyes are turning green with envy of Midget," Leila declared darkly, then showed her strong white teeth in a roguish smile. "Her father sent her this dream of a car from Paris. He's been painting at his Paris studio since early last spring. The roadster came the week after we left Hamilton. I was with Vera in their New York house. We were trying to decide what we should do to amuse ourselves until time for our trip here. Then the car came. We were so proud of it! We wanted the world to see it and us in it. We went on a motor trip to the Adirondacks. We stayed for two weeks with Vera's aunt at her camp. She was horrified because we came in the car without a chaperon. And I must tell you the truth! Neither of us remembered there was any such person to be considered when we started out with the car." Leila threw back her head and laughed.

"We didn't have one going back, either." Vera had caught what Leila was saying. "Luckily for us, my father thinks Leila and I can be trusted to take care of ourselves. We motored back to New York City and from there to Hamilton."

"So we did. And it's here we are stopping again, like a set of statues in the sun, when we might be on our way to the Ivy." By common consent the four had again grouped themselves on the walk opposite the roadster. "Come with me. Don't be dwadling here when there's news to be told and news to be heard," Leila rallied. She motioned Marjorie to the car and ceremoniously opened a rear door for her.

"Right-o!" Robin exclaimed, preparing to take the front seat of the roadster beside Vera. "I'm simply perishing for a real opportunity to talk. It seems ages and ages since college closed. Yet it is only a month. I have scads of things to tell you girls. Phil wanted to come with me. We had the trip all planned and her trunk was partly packed. Then three girl cousins descended upon the Moores for a visit. Poor Phil had to stay home and help entertain them. I'll tell you more about her when we are at the Ivy." Robin turned in the seat to say this much as Vera started the car.

As the roadster sped away from the station drive and swung into Herndon Avenue, Hamilton's main thoroughfare, Marjorie glanced slowly from one side of the street to the other. A happy little smile played upon her lips. Next to Sanford, her home town, she loved the staid college town of Hamilton. She loved it for its wide ornamental streets and stately green-lawned residences. Like all else which bore the name of Hamilton it seemed in some strange elusive way to partake of the fine character of its founder, Brooke Hamilton.

Presently she reached up and removed the white straw hat she wore. She gave a satisfied little intake of breath as the cool afternoon breeze blew gently in her face, lifting the thick clustering curls which framed it and blowing them back from her forehead. Her lovely features wore the untroubled, child-like expression which had ever made them so beautiful. Behind that beautiful untroubled face, however, was the resolute, indomitable spirit of a pioneer. It was that very spirit of endeavor which had made her a force for good at Hamilton College since her enrollment as a student of that institution.

After four years at Sanford High School, Marjorie Dean and four of her intimate girl friends had chosen Hamilton College as their Alma Mater. What happened to them as students at Sanford High School has been recorded in the "MARJORIE DEAN HIGH SCHOOL SERIES," comprising: "MARJORIE DEAN, HIGH SCHOOL FRESHMAN," "MARJORIE DEAN, HIGH SCHOOL SOPHOMORE," "MARJORIE DEAN, HIGH SCHOOL JUNIOR" and "MARJORIE DEAN, HIGH SCHOOL SENIOR."

The account of their doings at Hamilton College may be found in the "MARJORIE DEAN COLLEGE SERIES," comprising: "MARJORIE DEAN, COLLEGE FRESHMAN," "MARJORIE DEAN, COLLEGE SOPHOMORE," "MARJORIE DEAN, COLLEGE JUNIOR," "MARJORIE DEAN, COLLEGE SENIOR."

During Marjorie's senior year at Hamilton College she and her particular friends became interested in a plan to provide Hamilton students in less fortunate financial circumstances than themselves with suitable quarters in which to live. The fact that such students were making great personal sacrifices in order to obtain a college education had aroused the sympathy of Marjorie and her associates.

What began as the raising of a fund by which to make the way easier for the strugglers gradually led to a more ambitious plan on the part of Marjorie and her allies. They dreamed of a free dormitory for needy students which they determined by steady conscientious effort should some day be realized.

With the coming of Commencement which had seen Marjorie and her loyal supporters graduated from Hamilton College had come also the unexpected gift of a valuable piece of property as a site for the new dormitory. The donor, Miss Susanna Hamilton, was the great-niece of the founder of Hamilton College, Brooke Hamilton. While the eccentric old lady had been prejudiced for many years against the college board, she was, on the other hand, a warm friend of Marjorie Dean. During Marjorie's sophomore year she and Miss Susanna had met by accident. Later, Miss Hamilton had learned to love the sunny, gracious lieutenant. As a result of that love had come Miss Susanna's amazing concession.

During their senior year in college Marjorie and Robin had turned their attention to the giving of plays, concerts and other pleasing entertainments. These amusements had been welcomed by the Hamilton students and the two successful promoters had reaped a goodly sum of money for the dormitory project. The Nineteen Travelers, a confidential little band which included Marjorie and Robin, had also contributed several hundred dollars to the dormitory fund by the curtailing of personal expenses, elimination of all but a few luxuries and the practicing of self-denial in the matter of dinners and spreads.

The presentation by Miss Susanna Hamilton of the site for the dormitory had made the way clear for the erection of the building in the not far distant future.

At the time of her graduation Marjorie had been fully aware that hers and Robin's beloved enterprise would require their presence on the campus the following autumn. The real work of their project was yet to come. Robin was free to return to Hamilton. Marjorie had not been certain that her general and her captain would be willing that she should remain away from home another winter. She had left college for Sanford unable to assure her classmates who were to return the next autumn as post graduates that she would be then among them.

"So my prophetic Celtic bones did not lie," Leila said with teasing good humor. "Ah, Beauty, but was not Leila the wise Irish woman? Did I not prophesy that your general and your captain would be sending you back to college?"

"Of course you did. Your prophetic Celtic bones told you how utterly unselfish they were," Marjorie returned warmly. "We didn't exchange a word about my coming back as a P. G. while they were on the campus during Commencement week. One evening soon after we were home Jerry and Lucy came over and General said he had very important orders for the Army. He read us a ridiculous notice, ordering us to report at Hamilton College for post graduate duty, not later than October first, by order of General and Captain Dean. Jerry and Lucy made such a racket over it that General threatened to lock them in the guard house for boisterous conduct."

Leila listened, immensely tickled by Mr. Dean's army tactics. Marjorie continued to tell her of Jerry and her doings. She said nothing, however, of Jerry's brother. Entirely fancy free, Marjorie had never spoken confidentially of Hal to any girl save Constance. Jerry would not have ventured to ask Marjorie a personal question concerning him, intimate as the two girls were.

"Why, Leila," Marjorie said presently, going back to her superior officers, "after the girls went home that night I had a long talk with General and Captain. I found they considered it my first duty to come back to college. General pretended to be very threatening. He dared me to try to stay at home and see what would happen. I don't like to be away from them, Leila, but I love my work. And it's only begun on the campus. It will take us a long time to pay for the dormitory. I may be old as the hills by the time it is paid for," was her jocular prediction. "If I'm a tottering last leaf when that happens, at least I will have grown old in a good cause."

CHAPTER VII.
SCENTING MYSTERY

Vera was now bringing the roadster to a stop before the Ivy.

"Hello, old stand-by!" Marjorie raised a cheerful hand of greeting toward the familiar, one-story white stucco building. Its ornamental bungalow effect was made even more attractive by the traits of English ivy which wandered across the front of the shop and were trained above the door and the narrow-paned windows.

"Not another car parked here; glorious! This is a positive streak of luck!" congratulated Vera.

"The Ivy is popular with tourists this summer," Leila informed Marjorie and Robin as the girls sauntered up the wide white stone walk four abreast. "This is the first time since we came back that we have been able to park in front of the shop."

Entering the tea room they steered a straight course for one of four alcove tables. During the college year these tables were difficult to secure unless engaged beforehand. All four stood empty now. A brief lull in the mid-afternoon business of the Ivy had found the prosperous shop temporarily deserted.

"Who ever before saw an alcove table at the Ivy empty?" commented Robin as the chums seated themselves.

"It's almost as still here today as in chapel after Prexy has read out an amazing notice," declared Vera lightly.

"Observe how soon that chapel-like atmosphere will depart. We are here," Leila reminded.

"No; this beatific state of sweet silence is due to be shattered this very minute," Robin agreed.

"Right you are, Robin. It's a grand palaver we're about to have. Let us order the luncheon before the gabble party begins," proposed Leila. "Consomme, chicken à la king, potato straws, cucumber salad and whatever your sweet tooth demands for dessert? Yes?" She turned inquiring eyes on her friends. "And a pot of tea, of course?"

"It suits me. I wish I were going to eat that dandy luncheon this minute. I'm so hungry," sighed Marjorie.

Vera and Robin echoed Marjorie's wish. The waitress obligingly promised to hurry the consommé to the hungry quartette and retired briskly kitchenward.

"Now who is going to start the gabble ball rolling?" playfully demanded Vera.

"You and Leila. Tell us about the campus." Marjorie and Robin answered in the same words, and together. They both laughed. "One heart, one mind," Robin quoted.

"It's the same dear, green old stamping ground," Vera answered with proud fondness. "Only it almost gives one the blues to walk from one end of it to another without seeing any of one's pals. Now for news. Let me see. Kathie is coaching four would-be-freshies who are staying at Acasia House. They're in for entrance exams. Miss Remson has been away for a month, but she came back to the Hall the day Leila and I put in an appearance there. I sha'n't tell you a thing about Miss Remson's vacation trip. She wants to tell you herself. She said so."

"What an odd busy little woman she is." Robin smiled at mention of the brisk little manager of Wayland Hall. "I love her funny abrupt ways. She is so original."

"Jerry named her Busy Buzzy almost as soon as she first saw her when we went to Wayland Hall as freshies," reminisced Marjorie. "Muriel was quite fascinated by the name and those two villains went on calling Miss Remson Busy Buzzy behind her back for a long while. I was always afraid she might hear them say it, but thank goodness she never did. Muriel used to call Hortense Barlow, her roommate, Mortense. She and Jerry had the naming habit very hard that year."

Muriel's name brought a grin to Leila's face. "That rascal," she said with a chuckle. "What might she be doing these fine summer days? Is she coming back to college, Beauty? When we asked her last June about it she would tell us nothing. All she would offer was: 'I can't say. I'll have to think it over.'"

"She's still saying it," Marjorie echoed the chuckle. "She won't tell even Jerry and me what she intends to do about coming back. Jerry says she is only trying to tease us, but I think she has a reason for saying she is uncertain about it. She'll tell us when she is ready and not a minute before. Muriel has always been just so."

"I'll tell you all a bit of news," put in Robin. "Elaine is going to be married. Her engagement will be announced next month. She is——"

Three voices rippled an astonished "Oh-h-h." Three faces reflected the smile with which Robin had announced the news. Elaine Hunter, during her four years at Hamilton, had been the most popular girl at Silverton Hall.

"Who is Elaine going to marry, Robin?" asked Vera interestedly. "He'll have to be a wonder to be worthy of her."

"A delightful young civil engineer. His name is Kingdon Barrett. It is a real romance," Robin went on eagerly. "When Elaine was a tiny girl and this Mr. Barrett a small boy they used to go to the same beach every summer with their parents. They played together on the sand and were good friends. Then the Barretts went West and Elaine never saw her boy playmate again until Commencement. He was visiting Prexy's son and saw her name on the Commencement program. He actually picked her out among the graduates. The moment he had a chance he had Prexy Matthews, who knows her family well, introduce him to her. He told her who he was. They promptly fell in love and now they're engaged. Can you beat that?" Robin spread open both hands in a challenging gesture.

"We can not. Nor is it likely that we shall try. I have no wish to fall in love, for isn't it true that I might never be able to fall out again? It is a pit that I shall keep my feet well away from," declared Leila with unsentimental wisdom.

"I can't imagine you in love, you ridiculous girl," Vera's infectious giggle went the round of the table.

"Ah, if I were; and what a fine frenzy I should be in. Like this," Leila rolled her eyes, put on a lovelorn expression and struck her hand to her forehead with tragic force. She immediately rubbed her hand. "Arrah, but I have a hard forehead," she remarked ruefully.

The return of the waitress with the consomme put a momentary check on the animated rolling of what Vera had whimsically called the "gabble ball." The instant the hungry girls began their soup they resumed conversation. While Leila and Vera had many news items germane to the campus to relate, none of them were of moment. Robin had much concerning herself and Phylis Moore, her cousin, now a senior, to tell. Marjorie's news centered on Jerry's, Lucy's, Muriel's and her own doings during vacation. Of Ronny she had almost no news to relate. She had received but one letter from her since Ronny had sped West to her beautiful ranch home in California. The news of Elaine Hunter's engagement was, thus far, the banner surprise.

"Oh, girls, have you seen Miss Susanna since you came?" was Marjorie's concerned question, as the four lingered over the dessert of maple mousse and *petit fours*. "I've been trying to ask you that question from the first, and haven't."

"Now what makes you think we have seen her?" countered Leila with an elaborately innocent air.

"That means you have," Marjorie translated, "and you," she pointed an accusing finger at Leila, "and you," the finger moved on to Vera, "are trying to keep something from me. I know *you're* not guilty, Robin. *You* look innocent. But this pair look suspicious; oh, very suspicious."

"Now, Beauty, on your honor, do I look as though there was anything I could refuse to tell you, provided I knew it?" ingratiated Leila, her bright blue eyes a-twinkle. She appeared to be wrestling with a secret mirth which threatened to overrun her mischievous face. She now made mysterious signs to Vera whose smiles were also in evidence.

"You look too tantalizing for words. So does Vera. Oh, I know you both!"

"So you take us for a precious pair of rogues; eh, Beauty!" Leila made a smiling failure of trying to appear reproachful. "Never mind. Midget and Leila forgive you. Bring forth the mystic writing, Midget. May Beauty's bad opinion of us fly away on swift wings!"

CHAPTER VIII.
WHITE MAGIC

"So that's the reason for these nods and becks and wreathed smiles!" Marjorie made an energetic grab at the square creamy envelope which Leila was waving slowly back and forth before her eyes. "I'll assume it's for me," she said as her fingers closed around it. Leila purposely allowed the envelope to slip through her hand.

"Oh, it's from Miss Susanna!" Marjorie gave a little joyful cry. "Now I know you must have seen her. There's no stamp on the envelope."

"Might not Jonas have brought the letter to the Hall?" Leila suggested.

"He might have, but he didn't," Marjorie cannily retorted. "You've been to Hamilton Arms." Her eyes sparkled with the pleasure of her guess.

"So we have," Vera corroborated as though quite surprised at the fact.

"Yes, 'So we have,'" mimicked Marjorie as she hastily tore open the envelope and drew out the letter it contained. "I'm going to read you Miss Susanna's letter. I shouldn't, to pay you for teasing me. But, as Muriel loves to say, 'I'm always amiable when I'm not peevish.' I'm sure Miss Susanna would like you to hear it," she added more seriously. She began:

"Dear Child:

"How glad I shall be to see you again. I am looking forward earnestly to your return to Hamilton. I must remind you of your promise to spend at least a part of your time with me at the Arms. I am sending you my greetings and love by two trusted messengers. I wonder if you will be as greatly surprised and delighted to see them as I was? Will you come to the Arms as soon as you conveniently can after you arrive on the campus? Bring Robin Page and Leila and Vera with you. Pardon the fond impatience of

"Your devoted friend,

SUSANNA CRAIG HAMILTON

"How dearly she loves you, Marjorie," Robin said unenviously. "But then, how could she help it? So do we all. You have reason to be proud of having annexed the last of the Hamiltons to your train, Marvelous Manager."

"I had nothing to do with it. No one could annex Miss Susanna to anything," Marjorie disclaimed, shaking her head in sturdy fashion. "I always loved her from the first. She was like an odd, rare, lonely little bird to me. She was wonderful to me for her own dearness and still more wonderful because she was Brooke Hamilton's great niece."

"You've had nothing to do with any good work that has gone on on the campus in the past four years," Leila agreed with satiric emphasis. "So you say. Now tell me, which of us could have softened Miss Susanna's heart to the college? Never think you are not of small use in the world, Beauty."

"I decline to think of it at all," Marjorie evaded. "I'd rather think about when to go to see Miss Susanna. Why can't we go to the Arms today? We've had such a late luncheon. Suppose we hurry along to the Hall, see Miss Remson for a little while then go to Hamilton Arms? By that time it will be six o'clock and Miss Susanna will have had tea. We can stay with her until about eight and stop at Baretti's to dinner on the way to the Hall."

"Fine, fine!" applauded Vera, "more marvelous managing by M. M. Dean." At the same time, happening to catch Leila's eye the two exchanged significant glances which Marjorie intercepted.

"There, I caught you exchanging eye messages!" she exclaimed in triumph. "You know something I ought to know that you haven't told me." She glanced quickly at Robin. "No, Robin doesn't know this time, either."

"What is this odd talk I'm hearing?" Leila inquired guilelessly. "Have I a thousand secrets because I give Midget a friendly eye-beam?"

"That was more than a merely friendly eye-beam," disagreed Marjorie. "Besides, Midget had the mate to it ready."

"Did she, indeed?" Leila's black brows lifted with exaggerated interest. "You will have it that we are a designing pair. Only the stars know we're not that. My luck is poor." Leila sighed heavily. "How can I prove my words. Not a star will be around until tonight."

"You're worse than designing. You're a fake," emphasized Marjorie.

Leila received the assertion with the broad, ingenuous smile for which she was famed on the campus. "I believe you, Beauty," she said with an admiring candor which produced ready laughter.

"We ought to make a start for the campus, girls." Robin consulted her wrist watch.

"Away we go. Remember this is my feast." Leila was on her feet, the luncheon check in one hand.

"Remember the Baretti dinner is to be mine," Marjorie impressed upon her companions. "The Dean Entertainment fund *must* be used, you know."

"Don't forget the grand banquet at the Colonial tomorrow night," Robin announced in a managerial voice. "You're not the only person on the campus with an entertainment fund."

"My treat will be a dinner at Orchard Inn," Vera promised. "You two girls have never been to Orchard Inn. Wait until you see it." She grew enthusiastic. "Leila and I just happened to discover it while we were out driving. There; that's all I intend to tell you about it."

"Is not Midget cruel?" Leila shook a disapproving head.

"Is not Leila aggravating," retaliated Vera, imitating Leila's tone.

"Since you ask outright; yes, to both questions. We couldn't help thinking it, but we were too polite to say so," declared Robin. "We've a grievance of our own against those two. Haven't we, Marjorie?"

"I should say we had." Marjorie laid stress on her reply.

"Ah, no; you only think you have," retorted Leila.

A flash of familiarity came with the words "you only think you have," but to Marjorie's brain only. Now she remembered. That was precisely what Hal had said to her on their last boat ride when he had declared that she had never grown up. Her merry look, born of her companions' repartee, faded, to be replaced by a faint pucker of brow. To think of Hal meant to recall the hurt expression on his handsome features as she had last seen them.

Quick as they had been to seek the cool inviting hospitality of the Ivy, the re-united friends were now as eager to depart from it upon their light-hearted way to the campus.

"I'm going to hit up a pace," Vera slangily informed them, swaggering up to the roadster in an exact imitation of a racing motorcyclist she had recently seen.

Under her small practiced hands the smart roadster was presently whisking through the town of Hamilton at a rate just escaping that of speeding. Soon they had left the dignified town to its late afternoon drowsing and were skimming along Hamilton Highway. A short stretch of straight road then the highway began to wind in and out among the collection of handsome private properties known as Hamilton Estates. They were beautiful old-style manor houses for the most part surrounded by green rolling lawns and ancient trees.

"Oh, girls!" Marjorie called from her place on the front seat beside Vera. She and Robin had exchanged places for the ride to the campus. "Doesn't Hamilton Arms look wonderful? As if it were trying to show summer off at its very best."

"There's not another place among Hamilton Estates that compares with the Arms," was Vera's positive opinion.

"And why not? Didn't Brooke Hamilton plan it?" Leila made loyal demand. "Now maybe he knew Nature better than she knew herself. I have sometimes thought so."

"What a splendid tribute to him, Leila!" was Marjorie's admiring cry. "I must save that to tell Miss Susanna. How she will love it."

"Ah-h." Leila's affable grin appeared. "Now you begin to take account of my smartness."

"It seems almost unfriendly not to stop and go to Miss Susanna now, but I hate to disturb her before she has had her tea," Marjorie commented with concern.

"Don't worry, Beauty," Leila said. "We'll be coming back before long. We'll not 'phone her from the Hall. She has a taste for surprises. She only knows you are soon to be here. She'll be highly pleased to have you walk in on her."

"I'll surely do it," Marjorie returned with a decided little nod. She half smiled as she recalled a time when she had waited patiently to receive a summons into the eccentric old lady's presence. The peremptory invitation to appear at Hamilton Arms on a certain day to tea had filled her with the same sort of pleasant trepidation with which she would have received a summons to a royal court. Hamilton Arms was truly Miss Susanna's castle, where she reigned supreme, a lonely little chatelaine of a big house.

The smile still lingered on the lieutenant's lips as the car sped on and made the last turn in the highway before the end of Hamilton Estates was reached. Between the Estates and the campus of Hamilton College which had now come into view lay the strip of land on which was built the row of houses once used by the workmen who had erected the college buildings. Of the four occupants of the roadster Vera's eyes were the only ones turned away from the territory at the left hand side of the road. The other three girls were gazing in that direction with varying expressions. Leila's was purely mischievous. She was enjoying the amazement which Marjorie and Robin were showing.

"Why—what—who——?" Stupefied by what she was seeing Marjorie forgot to greet her old friend the campus in her usual devoted fashion.

Once, at this point along the straggling meadow road, dignified by the name of the street, had stood a shabby row of weather-stained houses. They had extended for a distance of what might be measured as two city blocks. An equally straggling cross lane divided the row almost in halves. Those above the cross lane looked more uncompromisingly ugly and faded than ever under the afternoon sun.

Those below the cross lane! Where were they? Where they had once stood were now huge heaps of broken brick, plaster, boards and the debris which always attends the tearing down of buildings. The ringing sound of many hammers in motion, the snapping of yielding wooden beams, the rattle of falling brick and plaster was in the air.

Above the cross lane the upper block of houses stood intact in its dingy loneliness. They appeared to frown upon the wreck of their companions of years.

Simultaneously Robin and Marjorie had raised a cry of astonishment. Vera promptly stopped the car in order to give them a chance to view the surprise at leisure. She dropped her hands from the wheel and with Leila enjoyed their amazement.

"Robin Page, can you believe your eyes?" Marjorie's voice achieved bewildered heights.

"Seeing is believing. How did it happen? That's what is bothering me."

"These two know." Marjorie turned in her seat, including Vera and Leila, in a comprehensive wave of the hand. "Now I understand what you two were so full of laugh about. I knew you had something else on your mind besides giving me Miss Susanna's letter. There's a new firm on the campus, it seems, Harper and Mason. And they've been very very busy!"

CHAPTER IX.
THE FAIRY TALE PRINCESS

"Never blame us," Leila said. "Weren't those houses but a rubbish heap the day we came, Midget?" She appealed to Vera for corroboration.

"Why, of course they were," emphasized Vera. "We thought you'd be surprised to see them torn down. We were."

"Surprised?" Marjorie repeated exultantly. "I'm simply amazed, astounded, dumbfounded, flabbergasted, stupefied by such a piece of good fortune. It's just what both Robin and I wanted."

"We worried during Commencement week because we hadn't the time then to see a firm of Hamilton contractors about having those houses torn down. You and Vera knew that, Leila Harper. You're implicated in this surprise somehow," Robin accused.

"My word as an honorable Irishman, I had not a thing to do with it," protested Leila, though she laughed.

"But you haven't said you didn't know who had. Never mind. I know. It was Miss Susanna. It must have been either she or President Matthews. He wouldn't have had——" Marjorie paused to think of a phrase which would describe the stately president's disinclination to intrude upon their project.

"The nerve," Vera supplied with a giggle.

Marjorie fell suddenly silent as she watched the busy workmen moving to and fro in their task of demolishment. The work, hers and Robin's great enterprise, had begun. She was thrilled by the thought of it.

"Time to be going, Midget."

Leila's voice broke into Marjorie's dream of the glory of work and the romance of worthy deeds. Marjorie could not tear her glance from the fascinating scene of labor. Yes; she and Robin had Miss Susanna to thank for this unexpected lift in their program.

"No one but Miss Susanna could have thought of this and then gone ahead and done it," Vera now said in a tone that partook of reverence as she started the car. "She wanted you and Robin to see what had been done as soon as you set foot in Hamilton. She told us to make it our business to lead you to it."

"Oh, wait until I see her!" Marjorie looked happy anticipation. Now they were coming into full sight of the velvety green campus. "Dear first friend, how are you?" she cried, stretching a hand of greeting toward the spread of living green.

Vera smiled in sympathy of the whimsical fancy. "You're as full of whimsies as Leila," she said. "She can almost convince one that Ireland is full of leprechauns and banshees."

From the beginning of the campus wall the distance to the central gates of the college was quickly covered by Vera's car. In the tonneau of the car Robin was still busy expressing her wonder to Leila of the surprise Miss Susanna had given them. Marjorie, however, remained silent as the roadster neared the main entrance. She was in the grip of many emotions. Her mind reverted to a day when she and her four Sanford chums had entered the gates of Hamilton College for the first time as explorers, seeking the treasures of an unknown region.

"Remember the stranger within thy gates," she was thinking. At first no one had "remembered" them, to their grieved chagrin. Then had come Helen Trent and then Leila and Vera. Their kindly offices had marked the beginning of fellowship at a college where snobbery had been the order of things instead of democracy which the founder, Brooke Hamilton, had made every effort to establish. Now, at the beginning of her fifth college year, she was returning to a Hamilton in which democracy had become a watchword. She experienced a swift exultation of spirit in thinking of the blessed change.

As the car passed between the massive stone gate posts Vera slackened speed and continued more slowly along the central campus drive. Came a turn to the left. Wayland Hall raised its handsome gray stone height only a few yards distant. Against the emerald of its short cropped lawn brilliant-hued verbenas, zenias and salvia flaunted beds of luxuriant bloom. Later in the season, cannas, gold and scarlet, and summer's queen, who arrives late, the ever popular dahlia, would have sway. Still later, hardy chrysanthemums would carry on the scheme of beauty.

Over one side of the veranda a late-flowering, creamy-pink climbing rose trailed its double fragrant clusters. At an end of the veranda purple and white clematis stars wove a mantle against a background of green. The spicy scent of garden pinks and tiger lilies was in the air. Wayland Hall rejoiced in a riot of flowers of which Miss Remson, its energetic little manager, took tender care. The buzzing of a select delegation of bees engaged in a honey-hunting expedition seemed the drowsing, humming voice of mid-summer itself.

On the veranda a small, wiry, familiar figure was watching the approach of the automobile and waving a preliminary greeting. Miss Remson's thin pleasant face grew brighter with welcome as she stood at the head of the steps, her eyes on the car as it slid onto the open space before the house.

Marjorie was the first one out of the car. It had hardly stopped when she skipped agily from it and ran toward the erect waiting figure. Miss Remson came half way down the steps to meet her and the two embraced with joyful vigor.

"My dear Marjorie, you are so very welcome. How I have missed you and all of my girls this summer." Miss Remson still held Marjorie's hands in hers. "So glad you are to stay at the Hall with Marjorie, Robina." She offered a cordial hand to Robin. "I am proud to have the illustrious firm of Page and Dean under my roof."

"And what of the firm of Harper and Mason?" demanded Leila. "Ah, there's a firm of note! Now tell me—where can you find it's equal?"

"Where, indeed?" was Miss Remson's question.

"They're a couple of bandits. They held me up behind the station and Lawless Leila snatched my bag," Marjorie accused. "While my supposed partner, here," she indicated Robin, "helped the daylight robbers."

"Shocking!" Miss Remson did not look in the least shocked. She entered into the spirit of teasing with zest. "I must be careful not to allow them inside the Hall. I'll have their luggage brought down and set out on the lawn. I had no idea I was harboring two such desperadoes."

"Arrah, don't be hard on us now!" Leila became coaxingly Hibernian. "You should be thinking of how lonely you were before Midget and I came wandering into the Hall. Had you even a long-faced, would-be freshie for company? You had not."

"I can afford to leave 'lonely' out of my vocabulary, now that I have some of my old household back again." Miss Remson exulted.

"And for that you may escort our old friend, Bean, as Leslie Cairns would have it, into the Hall," Leila graciously permitted. "Midget and I will be doing the same for our old friend Page." Leila possessed herself of Robin's traveling bag. Vera doughtily insisted on carrying Marjorie's bag.

"Set the bags in the hall, girls, and come into the dining room," Miss Remson directed as they entered the house. "I made a pitcher of tutti-frutti nectar, your old favorite, and Ellen baked three-layer cream cake this morning. Don't tell me you have just had luncheon."

"But we have," Robin said regretfully. The others swelled the chorus. Vera had an inspiration. It dawned while the tall frosted glasses were being filled.

"Let us drink Miss Remson's health in the nectar now and keep the cake for a spread when we come home tonight. Shades of the ten-thirty rule! We can't even remember what you sound like."

"There ain't no such animal," asserted Robin. "I thought we were to dine at Baretti's but the mind of this aggregation seems to have changed."

"That sounded like Jerry. Wish she were here. Giuseppe will have to miss seeing us tonight," Vera said lightly. "I'm in favor of a spread instead of dinner. I know the rest of you are or I'd have been drowned out with objections when I proposed it."

"The spread will be spread right here in the dining room," Miss Remson announced. "I'll expect you when I see you. You'll find me in the office. As soon as you're here the party will begin."

"You are as good as gold to us, Miss Remson," was Marjorie's appreciation. Taking up her glass of delicious amber-colored punch with its tempting dashes of plump scarlet cherries she proposed a toast to their kindly friend.

"We forgot to tell you where we were going, Miss Remson," Marjorie said apologetically when the commotion attending the drinking of the toast had subsided. "We're going to Hamilton Arms to see Miss Susanna. Robin and I feel as though we could hardly go there soon enough to thank her for her latest perfectly splendid kindness to us. You must know about it?" She fixed inquiring eyes on the manager.

"Yes; Leila and Vera told me. We thought you would go to see her first of all."

"I wish you were going with us," Marjorie said regretfully.

"This isn't the age of miracles," the manager retorted with dry humor.

"Some have come to pass. There are sure to be more some day." Marjorie chose to take this hopeful view. She knew of no two persons whom she would rather bring together than Miss Remson and Miss Susanna Hamilton. She wished each to discover and appreciate the other's manifold virtues. Miss Susanna, however, refused to extend her acquaintance on the campus. Aside from the two or three formal interviews she had had with President Matthews none but the nine girls who were Marjorie's intimates had been accorded her favor.

"Into the midst of the toast drinking now dashed a slender, brown-haired girl in a white linen frock. Her color ran high with happy anticipation; her eyes were dancing. Marjorie set her half-filled glass of nectar on the table in time to prevent a spill and gathered in the newcomer.

"Katherine Langly, and such a whirlwind! Who'd ever suspect you of being faculty?" she cried. "Leila was going to telephone you."

"Who told you to come here? Now I know you met a leprechaun hiding behind a tree on the campus and he whispered in your ear and slipped away." Leila looked uncanny wisdom.

"I never saw sign of one, but I did see old Amos. I was over at Wenderblatts and he came there to mow the lawn. He'd been mowing the campus just below the Hall and he told Lillian and me that he had seen Miss Dean and some more young ladies getting out of a car in front of the Hall. As soon as I heard I ran for the Hall. Lillian had callers so she couldn't come. She sent her dearest love." Katherine poured forth this explanation with an animation she had never possessed in her freshman and sophomore days at Hamilton.

Marjorie watched her in fascination. She was well content with the change in Katherine. Once she had been a sad, subdued, retiring mouse of a girl. She had now blossomed into a lively, high-spirited young woman. The youngest member of the faculty she was respected by her colleagues for her brilliant mentality. She had also won high honors in the Silver Pen, a literary sorority, as an author of unusual promise.

Kathie's arrival was the signal for a second round of nectar.

"I'll have to be it, much as I hate to," Vera presently mourned her tone particularly despairing.

"What is it you must be? Nothing your Celtic friend can save you from," was Leila's solicitous but rash promise.

"A time clock," sighed Vera. "I'm the only one of this fivesome who has any idea of the value of time. If we don't start for the Arms soon it may be Miss Susanna's bedtime before we arrive there."

"You must go with us, Kathie," declared Marjorie. "The more Travelers, the merrier. We're five of the old crowd, and I think it's great to have even that number together again."

"Of course I'll go. You don't think I'd let you run off to the Arms without me, do you?" Kathie's eyes sparkled with the gaiety of the occasion.

"We'd never do that; never-r-r!" Vera assured with a dramatic roll of "r."

"You must have known what Robin and I did not know until this afternoon," Marjorie said happily. "When were you at the Arms last, Kathie?"

"Last Tuesday afternoon to tea. Yes, I knew." Kathie flashed Marjorie a radiant look. "I was so glad. It was splendid in her."

Before Marjorie could reply Vera called out a second warning. "Shoo, shoo, shoo!" she cried, whisking in and out among her chums and relentlessly driving them toward the dining room door. Laughing, Miss Remson strolled after the fleeing, giggling girls.

The little manager was about to call a last word to the party as they began to descend the steps when the purr of an approaching automobile brought all eyes to bear upon it. One of the railway station taxicabs was now coming to a stop before the Hall. The instant it stopped the driver sprang from it to open the tonneau door. Next a girl in a silver gray dust coat and close-lined gray hat which suggested Paris emerged from the machine. She cast a slow unhurried glance toward the group on the veranda, then turned toward the driver in leisurely fashion and addressed him.

He dived into the tonneau, reappearing with a large leather label-spattered bag. The new arrival handed him his fare with the barest glance at him. He picked up the bag and started with it toward the veranda. She followed him, wearing an expression of such utter boredom it impressed itself upon the knot of girls to whom she was a stranger. One other point also impressed them. That point was her unusual beauty.

It seemed to Marjorie that she had never seen a girl so beautiful, and in such an unusual way. Her thick fine hair was like pale spun gold as it showed itself from under her small hat. Her skin was dazzling in its purity. Her eyes reminded Marjorie of the sea on a calm day. Only she could not be sure whether they were blue or green. Her features were not small but were admirably regular. She carried herself with the lovely, indifferent grace of a princess. Into Marjorie's fanciful mind suddenly popped the old-time fairy-tale beginning: "Once upon a time there was a lovely princess."

"Now whom have we here?" muttered Leila in Marjorie's ear.

Marjorie could not reply. The girl had reached the steps and was now composedly mounting them. She paid no more attention to the group on the steps than if they had not been there. She made an authoritative motion to the taxicab driver to place her bag on the veranda floor beside the door. She found the bell and rang it, looking even more bored.

As the stranger's fingers pressed the electric button Miss Remson stepped to her side. "I am Miss Remson, the manager of Wayland Hall. What can I do for you?" she asked courteously.

"Oh, are you Miss Remson?" She regarded the brisk, little woman with indolent blue-green eyes. Her sweet, indifferent drawl went perfectly with her unconcerned appearance. "I am Miss Monroe. You have my father's correspondence. I am here a trifle earlier than he mentioned in his letter to you. That need not signify," she added carelessly.

Careful not to intrude the Five Travelers had moved on down the steps and away from the Hall. Vera had parked the car farther down the drive.

"What a perfectly beautiful girl!" Marjorie softly exclaimed when they got out of earshot of the Hall.

A murmur of agreement answered her.

"I suppose she's a would-be," speculated Vera. "Still, she can't be. Miss Remson said yesterday that she didn't intend to take any would-be's until the week before the entrance exams. Then, only those who had applied for board at Wayland Hall. She never takes stray would-be's."

"Whoever she may be, she comes from afar," informed Leila shrewdly. "Her traveling bag is English, via Paris. She has the bored air of the English, but, set me down in the streets of Paris, and I'll soon be at the shop which furnished her hat and coat. If it is not one in the Rue de la Pais called L'harmonie, then I am no witch woman. The latest color plates they sent me show a coat like that gray."

"Perhaps she is a friend of Miss Remson's," was Kathie's suggestion.

As the five had not heard the brief exchange of words between the stranger and the manager they impersonally concurred with Kathie. Again hustled into the roadster by Vera they soon dropped the subject of the beautiful arrival at the Hall for the more personal one of Miss Susanna's gracious and unlooked-for help in the dormitory project.

Meanwhile, at Wayland Hall, Miss Monroe of London and Paris was lounging gracefully in a roomy willow rocker in the living room. She was appraising her surroundings through two limpid, but distinctly shrewd blue-green eyes and mentally ticketing them "not half bad."

In her office Miss Remson was frowning as she industriously consulted her letter file for the desired correspondence. The perturbed manager was very certain that she had not agreed to admit Miss Monroe, or any other strange young woman, to Wayland Hall in the middle of the summer.

She gave a kind of annoyed cluck as she finally found the desired correspondence between herself and the newcomer's father, who had signed his letters, "Herbert Cecil Monroe." They had been written from a Paris address and had been accompanied by satisfactory references. In them, however, her permission had not been asked, nor had she agreed to admit the daughter of her correspondent to Wayland Hall before the formal opening of Hamilton College.

CHAPTER X.
AT THE ARMS

"Where is she, Jonas?" Marjorie raised a cautioning finger. She hardly breathed the question for fear of Miss Susanna's proximity.

"She's up in Mr. Brooke's study, Miss Marjorie," Jonas replied in equally guarded tones. Miss Susanna's faithful retainer of years, the old man stood the center of the group of charming youthful visitors. He was smiling his vivid, crinkled smile as though he was thoroughly enjoying the invasion.

Contrary to expectation that Miss Susanna might be taking her accustomed stroll about the grounds after tea, the callers had reached the house without having seen sign of her. Jonas had answered their ring. He had come down the wide, thick-carpeted hall to the open door in his slow dignified fashion. His face had lighted beautifully at sight of the knot of bright-faced girls peering laughingly at him through the screen.

It was for Marjorie, however, that his smile was kindest. He shared Miss Susanna's fondness for "our young lady." The cordial handshake he gave her came straight from his worshiping heart.

"She's in the study quite a bit of late. *He* would have liked that." The old man nodded with conviction.

"I'm sure he would have, Jonas," Marjorie heartily agreed. Her chums smiled concurrence. They still had much of the same reserve for the courtly, silver-haired retainer that they experienced toward Miss Susanna. "We'd love to steal in on her there," she said with impulsive eagerness. "Do you think she'd care to be surprised in that way?"

"I know she would. Miss Marjorie." Jonas seemed very sure of this point. A faintly mischievous expression had leaped into his keen blue eyes. He surveyed her smilingly, as though debating something in his mind.

"What is it, Jonas?" Marjorie was quick to catch the change of expression.

"There's a sliding panel in Mr. Brooke's study, Miss Marjorie. Miss Susanna sits in Mr. Brooke's chair always when she's up there. Her back is toward the panel. I can let you in that way, if you'd like it."

"We'd *love* to." Marjorie grew radiant. She consulted her chums with dancing eyes. They made genial signs of wholesale approval. "Are you sure we won't startle her?" she asked as a prudent afterthought.

"She's not one to be startled," Jonas proudly assured. "She'll see you as quick almost as you see her. She's quick to see."

"Suppose I were to steal up behind her and slip my hands over her eyes? Perhaps I'd better not do that." Marjorie grew doubtful.

"Please do. She'd think it the best kind of fun," Jonas insisted. It was as though Miss Susanna were a child for whom Jonas delighted to provide entertainment. "She always says she likes adventure. She feels as though she'd had a good many adventures since she's known you and the young ladies here."

"We have had some real ones," Marjorie assured the old man. "All right, Jonas. We hereby appoint you as guide of this secret expedition. Lead on. We'll do our best to give Miss Susanna a wee little adventure. Not so little, either. A secret panel; that sounds thrilling."

"I'll put it in the first play I write for Page and Dean this fall," Kathie promised.

Led by Jonas the secret expedition tiptoed silently down the broad hall until they came to a lift. It was situated between the library and dining room and opened onto the second floor within a few feet of the study. It was seldom used by the energetic mistress of the Arms. Jonas opened its door without a sound and the five girls crowded into it, leaving him hardly enough space in which to operate it. At the second floor the man stopped the cage with a faint click and the adventurers stepped noiselessly, one after another, into the hall.

Jonas came last. He motioned the girls to follow him. Down the hall he walked, past the study and on to a small, railed-in balcony. The balcony adjoined the back wall of the study and formed a side of a little open square over the library after the fashion of a patio. Exactly in the middle of the balcony he stopped. The interested watchers saw him run a practiced hand up and down the severely beautiful wainscoting. Soundlessly, a smooth section of the wainscoting, between two raised edges, and fairly wide apart, slid to the left and disappeared from view. Its vanishment left an open space about three feet square.

Mutely peering into the study they saw Miss Susanna seated in Brooke Hamilton's chair. At the left of her, on the massive table lay a goodly pile of papers, yellowish and time stained. In front of her reposed another pile of official-looking papers and opened letters. She was too deeply immersed in a study of them to be aware of anything outside of them.

Jonas touched Marjorie's arm. He made a motion toward the aperture. She nodded in merry understanding. Stealthily she lifted first one foot, then the other, over the lower up-standing part of the wainscoting. Holding her breath she reached Miss Susanna's chair in two noiseless steps. Two soft hands found the old lady's eyes and closed over them.

"Who-o-o-o!" Miss Susanna cried out like a small tree owl. Like a flash her own sturdy hands readied up and caught Marjorie by the arm. "I know this game! I can guess who it is!" she cried out like a jubilant child.

"Guess, then," growled Marjorie in as gruff a voice as she could muster.

"Marvelous Manager," came with delighted certainty. This particular nickname for Marjorie seemed always most to amuse the old lady.

"Right-o! And who else?" Marjorie persisted, still keeping sight shut off from the chuckling victim.

"That's easy," boasted Miss Susanna. "Leila and Vera—yes—and Robin Page. Since you're here, child, she must be here, too. And Kathie. She's a fixture on the campus. Now drop those hands and let me have a look at you," impatiently commanded the old lady.

CHAPTER XI.
OUT OF THE PAST

The prisoning hands fell away from Miss Hamilton's eyes revealing five laughing girls clustered at one side of the historic chair in which the old lady sat, her expression one of keen enjoyment. She immediately held out her arms to Marjorie who slipped into them and kissed Miss Susanna on the forehead and on both cheeks.

"My dear, dear child. So you surprised me after all, though I have been on the watch for you. It was all Jonas' fault. He fixed up this scheme." Miss Susanna heartily returned Marjorie's caress with every evidence of affection. Next she motioned each of the others to her and kissed her on the cheek, a mark of favor they had not expected from the matter-of-fact mistress of the Arms.

"You stole a march on me, and Jonas helped you!" she exclaimed when the first babel of greeting had subsided. "I'm glad you found me here. I'm going to do something for you now that I think you'll like. Come, guess what. You made me guess."

"Show us something of interest that was Mr. Brooke Hamilton's," Marjorie made instant guess.

"Um-m-m; partly right," Miss Susanna put on a baffling expression.

"It's a letter, or one of those papers," hazarded Vera. "I mean what you are going to show us."

"Right again, but not altogether right." Miss Susanna was enjoying the moment of suspense.

"It's tea I can read in your eye, and I'll guess again it's been put off till this time each night this week," Leila slyly asserted. "Oh, I have a fine reasoning power." Leila showed her white teeth affably, "though there are those who do not believe it."

"Clever Leila!" Miss Susanna clapped her hands. "You've guessed the other half of my intention. I decided to have my tea late this week in case you girls dropped in on me. Kathie said that Marjorie would probably arrive when she came on the late afternoon train. I guessed the firm of Page and Dean would meet at the station," she said with humor.

"We did," Marjorie's light tone grew serious. "Oh, Miss Susanna, we *saw*, coming to the campus. We hardly know how to begin to thank you for the help you've given us. It means so much to us, who wish the work on the dormitory to progress, but even more to the girls who will live in the dormitory when it is completed." Marjorie had re-taken the old lady's hands in hers, pressing them gratefully.

Her friends and Jonas stood looking on at the fond little scene between the once crabbed mistress of the Arms and the gentle girl whose high principles and unfailing courtesy had won her the friendship of the difficult, embittered last of the Hamiltons.

"Never mind about that dormitory business now!" Miss Susanna held up an imperious hand. "I'll talk with you of it some other day—perhaps." She broke into a smile. "Jonas," she turned to the old man, "bring the tea up here."

"I used to have tea here occasionally with Uncle Brooke when I was a young girl," she told her interested guests. "He had tea promptly at half-past four every afternoon when he was at home, and usually in the study."

The Travelers listened almost breathlessly for her to continue. They were "positively greedy" for even scraps of information concerning the founder of Hamilton.

"All the tea he used was shipped to him from China. He never ate anything for tea except a few small, sweet English crackers. But how he liked tea! He would drink three cups, always. When I had tea with him he would have Jonas bring me the choicest marmalade and conserves, and little fancy rolls and sweet cakes. He would make an occasion of our tea drinking." Miss Susanna's face softened. She smiled reminiscently.

A pleasant silence ensued, broken only by the slight rustling of the papers on the table which Miss Hamilton was turning over. She drew from among the stack a long sheet of yellowed fine paper. It was spread open and written closely on one side.

"While we are waiting for Jonas to bring the tea," she said, an absent look in her eyes, "I will keep my promise and read you a letter that Uncle Brooke intended for the Marquis de Lafayette."

A sighing breath went up from the listeners who were now seated about the library table.

"It seems so strange; to know some one who knew someone else who knew Lafayette," Robin said wonderingly.

"So it does, until one stops to consider how long it was after the war of the Revolution before Lafayette came back to visit America. He came here in the year of 1824. Uncle Brooke was a very young man then. He was my great uncle, you must bear in mind. Lafayette was about sixty-six years of age when he made the American visit. He died ten years afterward. He and Uncle

Brooke corresponded regularly during the last years of Lafayette's life. The letter I shall read to you is, I imagine, the draft of a letter he composed to Lafayette. It is neither finished nor signed."

With this explanation Miss Susanna began in her concise utterance:

"My Dear Friend:

"How swiftly time passes! I can scarcely realize that almost two years have elapsed since you visited the United States. I had hoped to come to you in France, not later than next autumn, but a peculiar, and what I trust may be a fortunate, turn in my affairs makes it necessary for me to sail for China next month. It is my expectation to remain in China for at least a year and embark upon what promises to be a successful business venture.

"I am greatly concerned in thinking of you and of the future of my country. How little I gave you mentally and spiritually in comparison with all you gave me—the true essence of lofty patriotism; the counsel of a mind among minds. I shall ever keep before me your nobility of spirit; your boundless generosity to America; your unfailing consideration toward me. I am of the opinion that my best effort to please you must lie in helping my country. What does our United States need that I can give? My life? Always at call. Yet how else may I perform my patriotic part?

"Only to you can I confide an idea, recurring often to me since the death of my mother, which occurred when I was a boy of fifteen. She was an exceptional woman who, with her two brothers, had been educated by a tutor in England. She was a staunch advocate of the higher education for young women. I have never since known her equal. She, herself, being the strongest proof of her belief. Having known *her* can I, therefore, be less convinced of the grace and necessity of the higher education for young America's daughters as well as her sons.

"In loving memory of my mother I shall some day found a college for young women after my own heart. I have not much faith in polite female academies. My mind leans toward colleges for young women, conducted in precisely the same manner as are colleges for young men. Nor does it seem to me that the faculty of such institutions of learning should needs be composed entirely of women. The professors in our colleges for young men are far more proficient in learning than the majority of the women engaged to teach girls in the few seminaries and academies of the United States.

"In these painful, formative days of our republic young women should receive the same educational advantages as young men. Let us train them so that they in their turn may become competent instructors. Let not their budget of learning consist of a few polite ologies, lightly learned, to be as lightly forgotten. I believe men have better brains than women. Yet they lack in intuition. Women are keener of perception. Thus it would appear——"

Miss Susanna looked up from the paper. "That's all," she said abruptly. "I suppose he made a copy of this letter, finished it and sent it to the Marquis. I wished to read it to you because, in looking among his papers and letters, this is the first mention he made of his dream of building a college for women."

For a moment no one spoke. The spell of the unfinished letter of long ago gripped the hearers. The generous, purposeful personality of its writer made itself felt across the years.

Jonas, trundling a tea wagon into the study, brought them out of the historic past.

"How I wish we knew the rest of it," Marjorie said, her brown eyes childishly wistful.

"I wish you knew, but you never will," was Miss Susanna's crisp reply. "I've hunted for what might be a continuation of that letter on another, similar sheet of paper, but have never found it."

"It's a glorious letter, even if it isn't complete. It is full of hope and courage and resolve and conviction!" Katherine's tones rang with admiration.

"How beautifully he wrote of his mother," supplemented Vera.

"How well he wrote it all," was Leila's sweeping praise. "Too well not to have——" She paused. Carried away by impulse she had forgotten for the time the reason why the world could not have the history of a great man and his great work.

The sudden scarlet which flew to her own cheeks was no brighter than that which sprang into Miss Hamilton's.

"I know what you meant, Leila. Even a few months ago I would have been so cross with you for having said what you were thinking." Miss Susanna looked up from her arranging of the tea set on the library table and met Leila's eyes squarely. "I'm not—now. You may finish what you started to say." The permission was more like a half defiant command. It was as though the old lady had a sneaking desire to hear it.

"Too well not to have the world read it," Leila repeated. "It's of him I was thinking, Miss Susanna. He has a right to the high place he made for himself."

"I wish the *world* knew him as I knew him—but not Hamilton College!" the old lady cried out in petulant vexation. "I should be happy to publish his biography if I had not the college to hold me back. The Board is only too eager for information concerning Uncle Brooke. The moment the world received it, they would receive it, too. The members of that miserable Board would merely laugh at me because they had gained their point through me in a roundabout way. Whatever concessions I have made have been made recently, and only to please you girls. Most of all, to please Marjorie. My reasons for turning against the Board of Hamilton College were sound. Still, I know that in the same circumstances Uncle Brooke would have made allowance for their despicable behavior. But I am I, Susanna Hamilton, stubborn as a mule, so my father sometimes said. I can revere Uncle Brooke with all my heart, but I can't be like him."

CHAPTER XII.
IN LINE FOR TROUBLE

"Truly, Leslie Cairns, you make me tired!" Natalie Weyman clasped her bare arms behind her head with a jerk so petulant as to plainly convey her complete dissatisfaction. She surveyed Leslie, who lay stretched at ease on a brocaded chaise longue, with cold, displeased eyes.

"So you've often said," was the laconic return. Leslie did not even trouble to look toward Natalie. She was not in the least concerned at the ungracious opinion of her chum.—"Well, I mean it," scolded Natalie. "Why must you go running off to Hamilton in the very middle of the summer when we're having a good time here at Newport?"

"Glad you hail it as a good time," Leslie's plain, roughly hewed features relaxed from the stoical expression she carefully cultivated to a half satiric grin. "I think Newport's a dead burg this summer. Never saw such a collection of stupids gathered in one village before."

"You only say that," derided Natalie. "You've simply taken a notion to go to Hamilton. Goodness knows why. You're the most stubborn, obdurate girl!"

"I haven't asked you to go there with me, have I?" The questioned bordered on a sneer.

"I wouldn't go if you were to beg me to," Natalie flashed back.

"You'd go if I made a point of it," Leslie contradicted with assured insolence. She raised herself from the couch on one elbow and eyed her friend disdainfully.

"No, Leslie, I would *not*." Natalie seemed very certain on this point. "I'd not go within fifty miles of Hamilton College again after the way we left it. I really wonder at your nerve in doing it."

"Going to weep over one small flivver?" Leslie grew more ironical. "Forget it. You know how much I love to talk of it."

"I don't mention it very often," Natalie said bitterly.

"The less often, the better. If I hadn't business of my own to attend to I'd go after Dulcie Vale's scalp. Venomous little traitor!" A deep scowl did not add to Leslie's appearance.

"She's in Europe. She crossed on the same steamer with Joan Myers. She tried to talk to Joan, but Joan couldn't see her for a minute. I had a letter from Joan from Paris." Natalie volunteered this information.

"Hm-m. Looks as though she'd keep her scalp for awhile," Leslie observed with grim humor. "I'll catch her sometime—coming or going. What I'd rather do is hang around dear old Hamilton," Leslie put mocking sarcasm into the last three words, "and see what I can put over on Bean."

"What do you mean?" Natalie looked mystified. "What could you do now? Bean has a home, I believe. One would naturally suppose she'd go to it after having been graduated with honors at Hamilton." The bitterness of Natalie's tone indicated the jealous envy which mention of Marjorie Dean had aroused afresh.

"That's as much as you know about it. I happen to know that Bean will be in Hamilton and on the campus soon, if she's not there already."

"How do you happen to know it?" Natalie's face registered incredulity, then curiosity. Second thought caused her to remember that Leslie had ways of her own of finding out things.

"Never mind how." Leslie turned tantalizing. "'Nuff' said."

"I can't think of anything you could do to spite Bean. You tried your last trick when you bought that property you thought she wanted for her precious dormitory. What happened?" was the sarcastic retaliation.

"You'll never be celebrated as a great thinker, Nat," Leslie drawled, ignoring her companion's displeasing question. "Leave it to me to make matters hum for Bean. I'm going to Hamilton on the six-thirty train in the morning. I'll have something to tell you, you'd better believe when I come back."

"Oh, yes, 'Leave it to me,'" mimicked Natalie, an angry light in her gray-blue eyes. "You're crazy, Leslie Cairns," was her added scathing opinion.

"I'm not so much of a nut. What?" Leslie took no more umbrage at Natalie's rudeness than she would have at the buzzing of a fly. "Try to get it across your brain that I'm a business shark now, Nat. Will you?" she said with exaggerated patience. "I've sixty thousand dollars tied in a hard knot in that bunch of rickety shacks just off the campus. Those ancient corn cribs have to come down. What about my garage?"

"That for your garage." Natalie snapped contemptuous fingers. Leslie's insinuation that she was "thick" was the final drain on her patience. "You'll never make a go of it. It's too far from the campus," was her wet blanket prediction.

Leslie merely threw back her head and laughed in the noiseless, hobgoblin fashion for which she was noted among her few friends. Her silent, insolent merriment stung Natalie far more deeply than a retort could have done.

"Well it is." Natalie repeated, determined to hold her own.

The laughter died out of the other girl's face to be replaced by a lowering, bullying scowl.

"I tell you it is *not*," she emphasized in tones intended to forbid further contradiction. "Because it isn't in the same vicinity as the other garages is no sign it won't pay me to put up a garage on my new property. I'm going to build the kind of garage the Hamilton gang will cry for. I may run it myself."

"Wha-t-t!" In her astonishment Natalie half rose from her chair. She sat down again and gave Leslie a long-suffering glance, as if she could not credit what she had just heard.

Leslie was enjoying her chum's amazement. Of the eighteen girls who had composed the San Soucians, the club of girls who had been expelled from Hamilton College during their senior year, Natalie Weyman was the only one who had remained friendly with Leslie Cairns. The other members of the Sans, though betrayed into expulsion by the treachery of Dulcie Vale, chose to place the major share of the blame upon Leslie's shoulders. If Leslie had not arraigned Dulcie and ousted her from the Sans in their assembled presence, Dulcie would not have betrayed them. Or thus they argued. Leslie, who had been their leader, became a detested stranger.

While Natalie Weyman had cultivated Leslie assiduously at college because of her unlimited purse and flagrant disregard for rules, she had grown to like Leslie for herself. Because she was thoroughly selfish she inwardly approved of Leslie's calloused selfishness. After the Sans' expulsion from college she had not failed to keep in touch with Leslie.

At present she was entertaining Leslie at "Wavecrest," the Weyman's Newport villa. Leslie had arrived there only three days before with the drawling announcement: "I may stay, if you can rustle up some excitement." Natalie had gladly promised "the excitement" in the shape of a round of smart social events. Now with her plans nicely formulated Leslie had ungratefully taken it into her head to go to Hamilton.

"I'll say it once more. Be sure you get it this time. I may run my garage myself."

"You wouldn't." Natalie shook an unbelieving head.

"Why not?" Leslie coolly returned. "Think what an opportunity I'd have to keep a line on the knowledge shop."

"Why should you care what goes on there now?" Natalie cried in exasperation. "You're out of it, and ought to be glad of it. I am, I'm finding out every day that no one really in society cares much whether one was graduated from college or not. Smart schools for girls count for more."

"I care, but not in the way you think." Leslie suddenly swung her feet from the chaise longue to the floor. She sat very straight and viewed her chum somberly. "I don't care a hoot for Hamilton because it is Hamilton," she continued, her voice gruff. "It's Bean's performances that interest me. Not one of the Sans lost out as I did in getting the sack from Hamilton. I lost my father. He's the only person I know that I ever loved. I like you, Nat, even though we can't keep on affable terms five minutes at a stretch. But I *worship* my father." Leslie's heavy features went from merely heavy to downcast. "Bean is to blame for everything that went against me at Hamilton," was her sulky accusation.

"Oh, Les, you know that is ridiculous—to blame even that little prig for *everything!*" Natalie had truth enough in her shallow composition to realize the utter fallacy of such a statement.

"She was there, wasn't she? Well, then, what more do you want?" Leslie did not wait for her friend to answer her questions. "Bean was a disturber. I knew she would be the instant I first saw her. I did what I could to keep her down, but she bobbed up on every corner. Her crowd stuck to her; mine double-crossed me. She won; I lost my sheepskin and—my father. I'm not likely to forget that. She butted into the way the Sans had things regulated at Hamilton and tried to turn an exclusive college into a public school. She did it purposely. That makes her responsible, her and her Beanstalks, for *everything.* I chose to look at it in that way. So I'm going back to dear old Hamilton to mind my own business and maybe snarl up Bean's affairs a trifle. What?"

"You are foolish to think of such a thing. Stick to your own affairs and let Bean alone. *You'll* land in a snarl if you try to start mischief, Les." There was anxious warning in the advice.

"Save your breath." Leslie rose to her feet, her eyes on the jeweled watch encircling her wrist. "I'm going to hit the down. I must be up in time for the six forty-five train in the morning. Thank goodness I won't have to trail Gaylord along this time." Mrs. Alice Gaylord, Leslie's hired chaperon, had been graciously given permission to visit a sister while Leslie visited Natalie. Leslie had determined that she would make the trip to Hamilton alone, defying convention.

"When are you coming back, Les?" At the last Natalie gave in half amiably to what she could not change.

"Ask me something easier. It depends upon how long Bean lingers on the campus. I'm only going up there now to plan my campaign. I may not pull down my corn cribs till fall. As for landing in a snarl—not friend Leslie." She strolled to the door of Natalie's boudoir, where the two had been lounging. Hand on the door, she paused. "Bean is in line for trouble." Her heavy brows drew together ominously. "I told you I was a business shark. I intend she shall know it, too."

CHAPTER XIII.
AN UNGRACIOUS BEAUTY

True to their word the five Travelers left Hamilton Arms at a quarter to nine o'clock in order to spend a little time with Miss Remson before retiring. On the way to Wayland Hall the letter written by the master of the Arms in the heyday of his youth to the Marquis de Lafayette, his mature counsellor and friend, formed the chief topic of conversation.

"One might call that letter the cornerstone of Hamilton," Leila said thoughtfully.

"Yes," chimed in Vera. "Lafayette seems to have been the favored confidant of Mr. Brooke's magnificent idea. At that time many of the country's ablest men did not believe in the higher education for women. He was unique for those days."

"It was because he loved his mother so dearly that he could understand what a college would mean in the training of girls," was Robin's sober conjecture. "I hope he copied the letter and sent it."

"Oh, I am sure he sent it," Marjorie sprang into ready defense of her idol. "I imagine he always tried to finish whatever he set out to accomplish. Otherwise he could never have become the founder of Hamilton College."

"It seems strange to hear read a letter from one great man of long ago to another. Lafayette seems longer ago in time than he really was. My uncle has a letter which was written by George Washington. It describes a horse Washington offered a certain man for sale. The horse's name was Magnolia. My uncle bought the letter from a dealer in rare books and letters. I'll write him and ask him to send me a typed copy of it," Robin volunteered.

"Do; then I shall believe that Washington was no fairy tale. When I was a little girl didn't I believe that he belonged in an American fairy tale? It was my old nurse who told me that he was an American king who had cut down one hundred cherry trees at a stroke and who went to war in an invisible coat of mail so that he was never hurt. She had ideas of her own about him." Leila gave an enjoying chuckle.

It was the signal for more chuckles from her companions. It was difficult to say which was more diverting, Leila's droll remarks, or her inimitable manner of making them.

A brief lull in the conversation followed laughter. Marjorie broke it. She said with sudden irrelevance: "I'm not curious to know Miss Susanna's grievance against the Board. I only wish it could be adjusted. It doesn't seem right that Mr. Brooke Hamilton, who gave his time and heart and soul and spirit to such a noble enterprise, should remain a mystery. Miss Susanna feels so about it at times. She has said so to me. But there are more times when she doesn't; when she thinks only of her own grievance," Marjorie ended ruefully.

"That's the most I ever heard you say on such a ticklish subject, Beauty." Seated beside her in the tonneau, Leila laid a light hand over one of Marjorie's.

"I don't know whether it is the most I'll ever say, or not," Marjorie responded. "I'd rather not say it to Miss Susanna, but I would if I felt that I should," she continued with honest conviction.

Kathie, occupying one of the small seats of the tonneau, now leaned forward. "Professor Wenderblatt told me the other day that there had been several changes made in Board members since Miss Susanna's disagreement with them. I wonder if she knows it?" she said speculatively. "If she doesn't, and were to be told of it, perhaps it might make a difference in her attitude."

"I've never mentioned the Board to her. She has always spoken of it first to me, and then not often. I'm sure it would displease her if I were to speak of it first to her. It's too hard a matter for me to decide just now. She's been generous to Hamilton through us in the way Mr. Brooke would have been. I couldn't bear to displease her. It would seem so ungrateful. On the other hand, there's our Alma Mater. We children should stand bravely for her welfare," Marjorie reasoned loyally.

"I believe it will all work out for the best." Katherine was steadily hopeful of tone. "I think what Epictetus said about such conditions is consoling. He said: 'Do not choose to have all things happen as you would have them happen, but rather choose to have them happen as they will. Then shall the current of your life flow free.'"

"Thank you, Kathie." Marjorie's half pensive features brightened wonderfully. "That's an inspiring quotation, and I shall learn it this instant so as to have it handy to cheer me when I need to be 'chirked' up, as Delia our maid says. Please repeat it, and slowly."

Katherine obligingly repeated the quotation several times. Marjorie repeated it softly after her. Leila was so busy leaning forward, talking in Robin's ear she did not hear it.

"All passengers kindly get out of this car and walk. Step lively." Vera's voice, raised to a mild shout, broke in upon the bit of memorizing the two were earnestly engaging in. She had brought the roadster to a stop before the main gates of the campus and was now cheerfully inviting her companions to vacate it.

"A nice way to take us out to ride," Leila grumbled. "Are we not good enough to be carried to our own doorstep? What a treacherous disposition you have, Midget. Now I have found you out, and in time. I thank my stars." Leila left the car in her most leisurely manner.

"Oh, hurry up, slowpoke," giggled Vera, taking hold of Leila's arm to forward her progress from the car to the drive. "Robin likes my disposition. She hasn't found me out yet. She and I are going to take the car to the garage. Anybody else want to go, too?"

"Not I. I know when I'm unwelcome." Leila tossed her head with a haughty air.

Katherine and Marjorie, far from resenting the sudden order to "get out and walk" were already strolling slowly up the drive. Leila turned her back on Vera with a great show of scorn and overtook the strolling two. They found Miss Remson on the veranda, seated in a large willow rocker which made her appear unusually small.

"Back at last," she greeted in her lively tones. "What cheer? Was it dinner at Baretti's or tea at Miss Hamilton's?"

"Miss Susanna had a late tea on purpose for us," Marjorie replied. "Life has been one glorious succession of eats today since I got off the train at Hamilton station." This with an accompanying sigh of utter well-being.

"Don't forget the spread," the little manager reminded. "It's ready."

"So are we," declared Katherine brightly, "or we shall be when Vera and Robin come from the garage."

"No true Hamiltonite could resist a ten o'clock spread even if she had been lunched, toasted and tea'd," Marjorie cheerily asserted.

"No one could resist Ellen's cream cake, either. I know that," supplemented Kathie.

Vera and Robin presently returned and the quintette accompanied Miss Remson into the dining room where the "ten o'clock spread" awaited them. There was not only Ellen's delicious cream cake but dainty sandwiches and fruit salad as well. Though none of them were actually hungry, a spread was a spread on any occasion and therefore not to be passed by.

As they sat about one of the smaller tables, enjoying the little good-night feast, Miss Remson said with a kind of hesitating abruptness: "Girls, I have broken my rule of rules for the first time since I undertook the management of Wayland Hall. I have accepted a freshman far in advance of the regular opening of the Hall."

Interest flashed strongly into five pairs of eyes fixed on Miss Remson. The grim set of the little woman's jaw indicated her evident displeasure with herself at the departure from her few iron-clad rules. With the half chagrined admission came to each girl simultaneously a remembrance of the stranger they had seen in the late afternoon when leaving the Hall for Hamilton Arms.

"Do you mean the girl who came here this afternoon in a taxi as we were starting for the Arms?" Vera lifted the silence that had ensued after the manager's remarks.

"She is the one I mean." Miss Remson nodded slowly and without enthusiasm.

"The fairy-tale princess!" Marjorie exclaimed involuntarily, then laughed.

"She had that look, I grant you," Leila agreed. "Only it's from Paris she comes, and not out of a fairy tale."

"Correct, Leila. She arrived at New York City yesterday on a French steamer, and came straight from New York to Hamilton. Early last spring her father wrote me, applying for admission for her at the Hall to begin with the week before the opening of college and during her college year, provided she should pass her entrance examinations. Instead of abiding by the agreement which I made with him her father has sent her to the Hall several weeks too soon. There is nothing to be done in the matter save to allow her to remain. She tells me that her father sailed for Africa several days before she sailed for the United States. He joined an exploring expedition up the Amazon River." Miss Remson's face registered her disapproval in the matter.

"Don't worry, Miss Remson," Marjorie comforted. "We will take this would-be freshie under our august P. G. wings and bring her up a credit to Hamilton."

"The five Travelers to the rescue!" promised Robin with a wave of the hand.

Leila, Vera and Katherine were equally ready to extend a welcoming hand to the stranger from across the sea. Miss Remson surveyed her guests, a bright smile gradually driving away her annoyed expression.

"You girls are more hospitable than I. I ought to be ashamed of myself. I must try to live up to you." She paused, then proposed: "Suppose you go to her room and invite her to the spread? She has number 8."

"You're a jewel, Miss Remson." Vera patted one of the manager's hands.

"Nothing like social eats to promote acquaintance," nodded Robin.

"Come on." Leila was already half way to the door. "Let us visit our would-be in a body and speak to her as with one voice. What shall we say, so that we may all say the same, and not gabble at her like geese?"

"I don't fancy the concert invitation plan," Vera objected. "You do the inviting, Marjorie. You've a wonderful way with you."

"So have I," Leila hastily assured Vera. "Never forget that, Midget. I will praise myself rather than not be praised."

Laughing and joking the five post graduates hurried lightly up the stairs and down the second floor hall to room number 8. Nor when Vera knocked lightly on the door had it been decided as to which one of them should be spokesman.

The girl who answered the knock seemed lovelier to her callers than when they had seen her alighting from the taxicab that afternoon. She wore a pale primrose negligee which fell in straight soft folds to her feet. Its flowing sleeves dropped away from her white, rounded arms and the collarless cut of the negligee brought out the beauty of her shapely throat. Her peculiarly colored eyes roved from one face to another. They held a certain veiled inquiry not far from insolence. She was silent; evidently waiting for her callers to speak first.

"Good evening." While Marjorie had not consented to begin the making of friendly overtures with the prospective student she felt impelled to break the silence. "We are having a spread downstairs in the dining room. Miss Remson is giving it. Won't you join us?" she invited with pleasant directness.

"Oh, no, thank you. You could hardly expect me to come down *en deshabille.*" Contempt for invitation and callers lurked faintly in the answer; a contempt which the girls felt rather than heard.

"That need make no difference," Marjorie composedly returned. "There are no persons other than ourselves and the servants in the house. You know how purely informal a spread must be in order to be a success."

"I don't enjoy spreads," came the indifferent reply. "Besides sweets late in the evening are so hard on one's complexion." One of the blonde girl's white, beautifully kept hands found the door and rested against the knob. Whether by accident or design was hard to say.

"I am sorry you do not care to come," Marjorie said with the gentle courtesy which never seemed to fail her in the face of rebuff. "Pardon me for being so remiss. Let me introduce my friends and myself to you. Miss Remson has told us that you are Miss Monroe."

The indifferent expression on the girl's face appeared to increase rather than diminish. She merely stared at the group and said not a word. Marjorie felt uncomfortable embarrassment seize her. Nevertheless friendliness continued in her tone as she named her chums to the other girl. Miss Monroe had the grace to acknowledge the introduction. She nodded carelessly to each girl in turn, the air of furtive contempt which had visited her at sight of the callers returning.

"We should be glad to show you about Hamilton and the campus," Vera rallied to Marjorie's assistance. "We are visiting Miss Remson for a short time. We shall return to college in the fall and shall live at Wayland Hall. So we shall be your neighbors. Miss Harper's and my room is 10. We are using our old room now, and it will be ours again when we come back in the fall."

"I expect to try for the sophomore class." Miss Monroe crested her golden head. "I hope to escape the odious freshman class. I detest the bare idea of being kept down. Thank you for your offer to show me about." She favored Vera with an inconsequential smile.

"You are welcome." Vera tried to keep reserve out of the response. She did not enjoy being snubbed, either.

"You are sure to like Wayland Hall. It is the oldest and has been reckoned as the favorite house on the campus." Leila now broke into the conversation. "All of us except Miss Page have lived here since we entered Hamilton. We are P. G.'s." Leila gave the information in a perfectly level tone. There was an inscrutable light in her bright blue eyes which Miss Monroe did not miss. She colored slightly and hastily looked away from Leila.

Her remarkable blue-green eyes wandered to Marjorie again and rested curiously upon her. In that instant's survey she saw what she had not yet allowed herself to note. She saw a girl whose claim to great beauty was as strong as her own. The discovery did not contribute to her happiness, but she was too clever to allow even a shade of rising jealousy to cross her beautiful face.

"I suppose 'P. G.' stands for post graduate?" she returned with a questioning inflection. "I really know very little of American colleges. I am sure I shall find college such a bore. My father insists that I shall become a student of Hamilton. So tiresome in him!"

The five Travelers still stood in a half circle outside the door. Miss Monroe had no intention of inviting them in, it appeared.

"We've had the very happiest kind of times in college," Robin was quick to defend her Alma Mater. "One gets out of college precisely what one puts into it. You'll feel differently about it after college opens and everything is in full swing."

"If we can help you at any time to feel at home here, or can do anything for you to add to your welfare, please let us know. We were strangers here, too, once upon a time." Marjorie smiled sunnily at discourteous Miss Monroe. There was finality in her little speech. "Miss Remson will expect us back," she said to her companions.

"You are very kind. I daresay I shall get on here." Miss Monroe moved her shoulders indifferently. "I prefer France or England to America. Of course it's bound to seem very ghastly here for a while." Sullen discontent lived for an instant on her pretty features. Marjorie's friendly offer seemed to annoy rather than please her.

"Not half so ghastly as though you were condemned to an English private school for girls." Leila assured with a flash of white teeth which appeared the extreme of affability. Her companions read into it another meaning. They knew if the haughty newcomer did not that Leila was blandly watching the self-centered girl measure off the rope with which to hang herself.

"I don't in the least understand your meaning." There crept into Miss Monroe's voice a decidedly petulant note.

"I know that very well, indeed," Leila replied with smiling imperturbability. "I was born in Ireland and half educated in Europe; partly in England, partly in Paris. The other half, the more important half of my education I received at Hamilton College. The best I can wish for you is that you may find at Hamilton what I found. I shall be glad to make Hamilton seem less ghastly to you, if I can. Good night."

Leila turned away from the door. Characteristic of her was the virtue of finality. She could not dwaddle over a situation.

Her retreat was a signal to the other four girls. They made conscientious effort to say good-night as pleasantly as they had saluted Miss Monroe. She, on the contrary, began to show a first faint sign of interest in her callers. Leila's information caused the Irish girl to rise in her opinion. She decided that she might be entertained by a little further talk with her.

"Will you—er—won't you——?" She spoke directly to Leila's back as the latter continued to move slowly down the corridor. Leila did not turn her head. Marjorie, walking behind her heard and turned her face toward the girl in the doorway. Again Miss Monroe subjected her to a protracted, nearly hostile stare. Then she went into her room and closed the door with a force that was anything but indifferent.

CHAPTER XIV.
A TRIAL OF PATIENCE

During the few steps down the stairs and back to the dining room no one spoke. At the door Vera relieved her pent-up feelings by softly exclaiming: "Stung!" bringing one small hand down smartly upon the other. The unaccustomed slang from dainty Midget cleared the snubbed P. G.'s cloudy atmosphere with a soft chorus of giggles.

Miss Remson listened to Kathie's account of their defeated errand with "Hum!" "Why, the idea!" and "Too bad!" Kathie had not said a word to Miss Monroe save to acknowledge the introduction Marjorie made and "Good-night." She now simply repeated the conversation as nearly as she could, placing no unfavorable stress on Miss Monroe's rude reception of the quintette.

"The way Kathie has told you about our call is the way we are all trying to feel about it," Marjorie said earnestly. "As good P. G.'s we must overlook more than ever what we may think is out of place. Miss Monroe isn't used to American girls, I suppose. Perhaps she thinks we are too eager, or that we haven't elegant repose, or——" She glanced inquiringly at her friends: "I don't know what she thinks."

"Let me say it for the rest of you. I have known a few like this girl in England, but none so pretty. She will be pleasant? Ah, yes; but who knows when?" Leila flashed a canny smile. "She did not ache to know us tonight. Her taste will not have improved by tomorrow; nor for many a long day."

"Never mind; we're not sensitive plants," was Marjorie's light assurance. "Our haughty, fairy-tale princess may change her mind about us later." Marjorie made light of the snub in order to soothe Miss Remson's wounded pride at the rudeness offered her favorite students. "Maybe she is so upset over having to come to America to college, when she doesn't wish to, that she can't be very cordial to any one."

"Good little Lieutenant, you keep the first tradition better than I." Leila dropped a fond arm over Marjorie's shoulder.

"Certainly, I don't, silly." Marjorie's energetically protesting tones suddenly ceased.

Silvery and sweet on the scented night air came the chimes' familiar prelude. Followed the stroke of eleven, clear, solemn, individual in tone. To Marjorie it was as though her second Hamilton friend had come to say a soothing good-night to her after a "trying hike." While she had kept on a strictly even keel during the short call on Miss Monroe she had secretly winced at the other girl's insolent reception of her and her chums.

While the chimes sang away the hurt she sat listening to them and trying to clear her brain of all ungenerous thoughts. Her face burned as she recalled the steady way in which Miss Monroe had looked at her. She understood the reason. While Marjorie was absolutely without vanity, she could not pretend that she did not know her own claim to beauty. For four years she had been hailed frankly at Hamilton as the college beauty. Far from flattered, she ducked the title whenever she could. Always in her mind lived the quaint charge delivered by the judge at the beauty contest which she had won during her freshman year.

"Brede ye, therefore, sweet maid, no vanitye of the mind, but say ye raythere, at even, a prayer of thankfulnesse for the gifte of Beauty by the Grace of God."

Strangely enough the ancient sentiment had popped into her mind at sight of beautiful, golden-haired Miss Monroe. With it had come a kindly plan of her own. She promised herself that she would put it into action as soon as she came back to Hamilton in the fall.

As a result of Miss Hamilton's energetic effort on behalf of Page and Dean, the willing firm found themselves more willing to work than overcrowded with it. More the secretive old lady ordered Marjorie and Robin to do nothing but have a good time with their chums for the next three days and not dare to come near the Arms or even call her on the telephone. Her emphatic message to them was:

"Come to the Arms to seven o'clock dinner, all of you, next Sunday evening. That means be at the Arms by three in the afternoon. Perhaps you may hear something to your interest."

Robin and Marjorie had not yet been nearer the cherished site than the point on Hamilton Highway from which they had viewed it on the day of their arrival on the campus. They delicately refrained from examining the work at close range until they had talked with Miss Susanna and received her sanction.

"We can well afford this layoff," Robin had blithely declared to Marjorie. "Thanks to Miss Susanna we're miles farther ahead with this work than we dreamed of being." Marjorie patiently agreed with her though the two laughed as each read the longing for action in the other's face. The promoters were brimming with the buoyant impulse of youth. They yearned to get directly in touch with the big doings on the newly purchased property. Absolute belief that Miss Susanna had done better for the enterprise than they could have done had served to put a loyal curb on their natural impatience.

Meanwhile the five Travelers were deriving untold satisfaction from their reunion. Kathie's mornings and early afternoons were occupied in coaching her aspiring freshmen. She could always be counted upon for late afternoon and evening. Leila and Vera had nothing to do save please their chums, incidentally pleasing themselves. Marjorie and Robin talked importantly about being "laid-off" and took occasion to make the most of it.

Sunday afternoon saw them leaving the campus in Vera's car, radiant with health and good looks, which their delicate summer finery intensified. A "bid" to the Arms was always a red letter occasion. They were bubbling with light-hearted satisfaction. Miss Susanna, seated in a high-backed rocker on the ivy-decked veranda, appeared to catch the spirit of their gaiety. She got up from her chair and waved a book she had been reading in energetic salute as the roadster rolled up the drive. She was wearing a soft white silk dress, turned in a little at the neck and fastened with a priceless cameo pin, oval and set with a double row of pearls and rubies.

"Now doesn't she look like the pleased old child?" Leila murmured to Marjorie as they left the car.

Marjorie had time only for a quick nod. She quite agreed with Leila. The touch of grimness usually present on Miss Hamilton's face had given place to a childishly happy look which was good to see.

No one of the five Travelers were ever likely to forget that particular afternoon chiefly because of the peculiarly charming "youngness" of spirit exhibited by Miss Susanna. It fascinated them all. It was as though she had gone back over the years to girlhood.

They spent the afternoon out of doors, at first roving about the magnificent breadth of lawn with their vivacious guide. She had plenty of interesting bits of the history of the Hamiltons to relate, called to mind at sight of a particular tree, shrub or nook of special vernal or floral beauty.

Later, they gathered in a quaint Chinese pagoda set in the midst of a group of graceful larches. There Jonas brought them tea and sweet crackers, all Miss Susanna would allow them to have on account of the approaching dinner hour. While they sipped the finest Chinese tea and nibbled crackers she told them of how Prince Tuan Chi, a Chinese noble and a friend of Brooke Hamilton, and her great uncle had themselves built the pagoda during a summer the young Chinese lord had spent at Hamilton Arms.

"All that happened before my time," Miss Susanna concluded with a sigh. There was a far-away gleam in her bright dark eyes. "Uncle Brooke used to tell me such tales when he and I took our walks about the Arms. Sometimes he would choose to walk with Jonas instead of me. Jonas was like a younger brother to him. How hurt I used to feel," she declared with a smile of self-mockery.

Thus far she had made no mention of the topic dear to Robin and Marjorie. Each time she spoke, in her crisp enunciation they pricked up mental ears. Each time they were doomed to vague disappointment. Still they could not fail to treasure every word she related concerning their idol, Brooke Hamilton.

"What time is it, Marjorie?" Miss Susanna finally asked. She cast a glance at the sun making its leisurely descent down the western sky. "My guess is—let me see—ten minutes past five."

"It's seven after. I should say you can guess time!" Robin opened surprised eyes. "Beg your pardon, Marjorie," she apologized. "I know you're not dumb."

"Considering you are Page and I am Dean, I'll forgive you," Marjorie assumed an important air. "Aren't the firm of Page and Dean one?"

"They are," Robin replied solemnly as though taking a vow.

"Which reminds me," broke in Miss Susanna, "that I have some business to transact with this distinguished firm, even if it is Sunday." There was a suggestion of eager stir in her announcement.

Marjorie felt an all but irresistible desire to ejaculate "Ha-a-a!" in one long relieved breath. It was coming at last. Robin wished she dared steal one glance at Marjorie. Instead she sat very still, a faint-breathing figure of expectation. Leila, Vera and Katherine watched Page and Dean and smiled. They, and they alone, knew how great had been the suspense of the promoters. Leila, ever full of fancy and mysticism wondered imaginatively if, somewhere in a world of light beyond the stars, Brooke Hamilton lived and watched with approval the carrying on of his beloved work.

CHAPTER XV.
OUT OF THE NIGHT

"What I have to say is particularly for Page and Dean though any and all Travelers are welcome to hear it," Miss Susanna's bright, bird-like eyes danced as she fondly surveyed her flock. A spot of vivid pink had appeared high on each cheek. She was like a youngster about to make a special confidence.

"To begin with," she said, "it was not my business to meddle with the affairs of Page and Dean. I have no excuse to offer. I meddled because— well—I felt the need of meddling. Jonas egged me on. He's every bit as much to blame as I." She gave the gleeful chuckle which the girls loved so much to hear. "You two rising promoters did not know a certain man I know, and have known for years. Perhaps he is my real excuse for meddling." The little old lady tilted her head reflectively to one side.

"That man is Peter Graham," she continued. "The Grahams are one of the old Hamilton families. Peter Graham's wife, Anne Dexter, and I were chums. I was Anne's sole attendant when she married Peter. They never achieved riches as Uncle Brooke did. They were lucky in love, but have been unlucky in business. Peter is still a builder, graduated from a carpentership. As a young man he wished to study architecture. Then he married and lost track of his ambition in trying to be a creditable family man. He had a natural genius for planning houses and large buildings and did well when he could secure a contract. Hamilton is chiefly made up of old houses, mostly colonial, and staunchly built. I used to advise Peter to go away from here and establish himself in a large city where contracts were more plentiful, but Anne did not wish to leave Hamilton. Once I offered to help him and hurt his feelings dreadfully. When you talked of building a dormitory I did not at first think of Peter. After you girls had left here last June it flashed across me one afternoon as I was taking my walk that Peter's chance had come at last."

An audible breath of approval ascended from the attentive listeners. They were already deeply enough interested in Peter Graham to be in sympathy with his upward struggle.

"I knew I could trust Peter to give you his best in all ways," was the positive declaration. "His bid for the entire operation—tearing down the old houses, preparing the site for the new building and erecting the dormitory was moderate in comparison with the figures I received from two widely known firms of builders. As you children have resolved to clear away the debt you will incur in building the dormitory you can do no better than trust the operation to Peter Graham. Jonas agrees with me. At first I thought of writing you about it, Marjorie. I found I did not feel like writing. I decided to tell you and Robin when you came to Hamilton. Time was flying, with nothing done. I sent for Peter and told him what I wanted. I made him happy. I know you are pleased with the progress he has made. But I don't know what you think of Jonas and me." She stopped with a half embarrassed laugh.

"There is only one thing we could think." Marjorie's face glowed with devotion. "You and Jonas must feel about Hamilton as Mr. Brooke Hamilton felt. You'd have to, in your heart, or you couldn't have done such wonderful things for the students to come."

"No such thing," contradicted the old lady in an odd, harsh voice. "I mean, the way I feel about the college. Jonas is Uncle Brooke's man, heart and soul. He still nurses all of Uncle Brooke's plans for Hamilton College. Let us have it understood, here and now, that if a dear little friend of mine, Marjorie Dean, had not interested me in the plucky way she and her chums were fighting to turn that snob shop on the campus into a democracy, I'd not have lifted a finger for the benefit of Hamilton. As it turned out, Marvelous Manager's way was his way. So I managed to please both," she ended, her tone softening.

"Truly, Miss Susanna, that is the nicest compliment I ever had." Marjorie showed such obvious delight at being ranked with the man she so reverenced that Miss Susanna's own crinkly smile broke forth.

"Glad you liked it." She continued to smile. Marjorie regarded her eccentric benefactor with utter devotion. Miss Susanna was flowering forth into graciousness as a peach tree breaks forth into rosy bloom in early spring. The others were watching the devoted pair and smiling their approval.

"You had better come to tea tomorrow afternoon, Robin and Marjorie," Miss Hamilton now invited. "I'll send for Peter Graham to come, too. Then you can talk matters over with him. There'll be no papers to sign. Our word is as good as Peter's and Peter's is as good as ours. Don't cry because you're not invited to tea," she humorously consoled the uninvited trio. "I'll invite you to tea one of these fine days and leave out Page and Dean."

"You wouldn't be so mean," protested Robin.

"Wait a while and see," teased Leila, nodding with lifted brows at Page and Dean.

Having confessed her part and Jonas' in starting the building of the dormitory ahead of time, Miss Susanna had a great deal more to say on the subject. When Jonas came to remove the tea things she sent him to the house for a bundle of plans and specifications. These she spread out on the rustic table and began an explanation of them to her young friends.

"There'll be some water color drawings for you to see before long," she made lively promise. "Peter will do them himself. He is very clever in that line."

In spite of the fact that the supposedly crabbed mistress of Hamilton Arms mingled little with the business world she had a shrewd practical idea of values. She had listened carefully to her old friend, Peter Graham, when he had gone over the plans and specifications with her. Now she was ready to pass the information she had gained on to the five Travelers. So absorbed were they in listening as she unfolded the cherished enterprise to them they lost all idea of time. Jonas' deep gentle announcement: "Dinner time, Miss Susanna," reminded them that afternoon had slipped into evening.

It seemed to them that the end of a perfect day had indeed arrived when Miss Hamilton led the dinner procession of three couples into the tea room instead of the dining room. More, she explained that Jonas was proficient in Chinese cookery. Under his direction the cook would serve them with a real Chinese dinner.

It began with shark-fin soup and celery hearts, went triumphantly on through chicken mushroom chop suey, chow mein, rice, cooked as few other than the Chinese can cook rice, and costly Chinese tea. It ended with a very sweet dessert of preserved kumquats, crystalized ginger, almond cakes and barley candy. Jonas had spent the greater part of the day preparing the feast from recipes which he, Brooke Hamilton and the young Chinese lord, Prince Tuan Chi, had tried out with laughter and good cheer in the immense old-fashioned kitchen of the Arms.

After dinner Miss Susanna martialed the girls into the music room to sing for her. Robin was immediately besieged by all to sing.

"Oh, no," she demurred. "I'll play for all of us to sing." She began to play softly a song they all knew. They could not resist the lilt of it so they sang in concert. Several others, equal favorites followed.

"I've struck," Marjorie declared at the end of a fascinating waltz song from a recent musical success. "Not another note."

"So have I." There was an understanding glint in Leila's eyes. She rolled them meaningly at Vera and Katherine, then toward Robin. Two more reinforced the strike. Robin gave in and soon her glorious high soprano was filling the room with melody. She sang several of Miss Hamilton's favorite selections from grand opera. Then she balked, insisting that each of the others should contribute a solo.

Miss Susanna gave a sudden funny little cackle of laughter and agreed to do her part. The strikers could do no less. Each performer was to play her own accompaniment. "If you can't play it, play at it," stipulated Robin.

Leila came first with what she announced was an old Irish chant. The accompaniment had a great deal of heavy rumbling in the bass, the chant rose in a heart-rending wail which threatened with every succeeding note to burst bounds and become a wild howl. It was finally drowned in a gale of laughter as Jonas, not understanding the situation, suddenly appeared in the doorway, amazement written on his face.

Vera sang "Sweet and Low" so prettily she was encored and sang a baby song she had learned in the kindergarten. Her lisping baby accents set the party to laughing afresh. Katherine sang a charming little song she had learned in first year Greek. Marjorie sang "Won't you walk a little faster?" from "Alice in Wonderland," to a tune which her general had fitted to Carroll's immortal words when she was a youngster. It so charmed her hearers that within twenty minutes they were caroling "Will you, won't you?" in gleeful chorus.

Miss Susanna, however, contributed the star selection. She sat down before the piano with a good deal of chuckling, played a kind of rambling prelude and in a light, but tuneful voice proceeded to sing of the woes of one, Lord Lovell. According to the song, which was composed of many sing-sing verses, each ending with a ridiculous repetition of the last word of the last line, Lord Lovell was extremely unlucky in love. The longer she sang, the wilder grew the mirth of her audience. The final "spasm," as Miss Susanna afterward named it, told of the untimely death of both Lord Lovell and his lady fair and of how they were buried in one grave with sweet briar bushes planted above them. According to the song:

"The sweet briars grew till they reached the church top;

And there they couldn't grow any higher;

And so they formed a true lovers' knot,

Which all true lovers admire-rire-rire;

Which all true lovers admire."

It was after ten o'clock when the concert ended and half past ten before the Travelers had said good-night to the mistress of the Arms and were on the road to the campus. They had left Miss Hamilton, gay and smiling, immensely inspirited by their visit.

Vera had asked Leila to take the wheel going to the campus. "I want to be a lady instead of a chauffeur for a change," she plaintively explained to Leila.

"It takes more than sitting on the back seat of the car resting your hands and face to be a lady, Midget," was Leila's discouraging response.

Marjorie had elected to ride beside Leila. The two girls were trying to remember the words and at least part of the tune of "Lord Lovell." Robin had said that she thought she could arrange it as a funny quartette. Miss Susanna had offered to find the music to it in an old book of hers.

"Look out, Leila; here comes a car, and fast, too," Marjorie warned in a low tone. They were at the narrowest part of the highway which lay between them and the campus.

Leila had already seen the approaching car and was keeping her own side of the pike strictly. Came a flare of white lights. Marjorie cast an alert but incurious glance at the other car. She drew a sudden audible breath and said softly, but sharply: "Leila, did you see who was in that car?" In the same instant the car to which she referred glided on into the darkness of the summer night. Quickly as it had passed their automobile Marjorie had had a full glimpse of the driver of the other car. A young woman had the wheel whose dark irregular features were only too familiar. For reasons best known to herself, Leslie Cairns had returned to Hamilton.

CHAPTER XVI.
ENCHANTED?

During the busy days which followed the dinner with Miss Susanna, the firm of Page and Dean proved themselves worthy of the name promoters. Their first meeting with Peter Graham was the beginning of earnest daily consultations with him. Not a day passed that did not find them on the ground where their work was going steadily forward. They were a wise pair of promoters who left the management to Mr. Graham and never annoyed him by interfering with his arrangements. Part of the workmen were from the town of Hamilton, the other part from a colony of dark-faced foreigners who lived in the eastern section of the town.

Robin declared enthusiastically after her first morning spent at the site that just to see the men at work was inspiring. The minds of the two young women had been trained to grasp the principle of a problem or operation. It was not long before they had become familiar with the work in hand and understood much of it in detail.

Peter Graham was quietly happy over the rapid progress which was being made in the demolishment of the row of old houses. For years he had waited and longed for "a big chance." Now it had come. He was devoted hardly less loyally to the building of the dormitory than were Robin and Marjorie.

Leila and Vera spent the days thinking up pleasant amusements for Page and Dean's leisure hours. They were usually on hand with the roadster to take the pair of promoters to and from the site and for long drives afterward. They simulated a respect for Page and Dean which was flattering, but not genuine. They gave each other much loud advice about breaking in on a rising firm during business hours. Neither followed either her own or the other's caution.

Since their kindly but unsuccessful attempt to welcome Doris Monroe to Wayland Hall and Hamilton College, none of the Travelers had ventured further friendly overtures. The four girls at the Hall breakfasted early. Miss Monroe invariably breakfasted as late as she could before the close of the breakfast hour. Once or twice they had met her sauntering into the dining room as they were leaving it.

A half smiling, indifferent nod, intended to include the four was indicative of her lack of interest in her recent callers. Occasionally one or another of the chums would chance to encounter her about the Hall or on the campus. She met them with the same slighting manner; only a remove from discourtesy.

"Miss Monroe of London and Paris has the manners of neither," Leila delivered this unflattering opinion of the aloof student one Sunday afternoon. The chums had just encountered Miss Monroe on their way toward the east gate and the garage. "She is as rude as Leslie Cairns used to be. What a fine time the two could have together. One has no more politeness than the other."

"She is so lovely, even though she isn't a tiny bit cordial," Marjorie said charitably. "It seems too bad that we can't find a way to charm our fairy-tale princess."

"Let her strictly alone," was Leila's succinct advice. "She would not be grateful to us for our trouble."

"I can't help agreeing with you, Leila," Kathie said frankly. "Later she may thaw and decide she would like to know us. If that should happen, we're not small-souled enough to resent past snubs."

"Neither do we belong to the Royal Order of the Doormat," Leila retorted. "She will have to turn most gracious if my wounded Irish pride is to be soothed." Leila's accompanying grin indicated precisely how greatly her sensitive Irish pride had been hurt.

"Do let us talk of something more interesting than that enigma," Vera said with a patient sigh. "Why she should treat four learned P. G.'s and a member of the faculty as though they were presuming freshies and she a senior is something I shall not attempt to puzzle out. Where to this afternoon, children? How about straight north on Hamilton Highway with an evening stop for dinner at Orchard Inn?"

A chorus of "Fine"; "Bully"; "Ducky" and "Right-o," rose in answer to her solicitous inquiries.

"Oh, dear; I wish I didn't have to go home Wednesday," came rather disconsolately from Marjorie. "I'm anxious to see Captain and General; as anxious as can be. But the work here is so fascinating!"

"I don't admire your choice of subject, either," Vera declared critically.

"All right. Miss Midget Mason. I'll try not to mention it again," Marjorie obligingly promised. "You seem to be another sensitive soul; something like Celtic Leila."

"Oh, I am," Vera assured, then out rippled her merry little laugh. "Vera's Own Variety," Marjorie had playfully named it.

"I'm overdue at home now. Can't help it if the subject is painful to you, Midget. I have to say that much."

"Marjorie has a date with her superior officers. Robin's overdue in Virginia. Two plus two make four. And the moral of that little sum, my dears, is: What's the use in teasing 'em to stay?" propounded Kathie.

"What, indeed? Since Robin must go and Kathie must stay what is to become of Midget and me?" Leila's attempt at looking forlorn was short-lived. She could not keep a sober face.

"Now what do you know that I don't?" Marjorie demanded. Leila's smiles were directed to her.

"Listen to the witch woman, Leila." The Irish girl reached for one of Marjorie's hands and peered at the pink outspread palm. "You are going on a journey——"

"Of course I am. I know that. Tell me something I don't——"

"Treat the seeress with more respect. You are going on a long journey in a car. Might it not be a roadster? You——"

"Oh, see here. I can tell my own fortune as well as that," objected Marjorie.

"Not yet. Now be more civil. I am no ordinary person," Leila rebuked. "On this journey you will be in the company of a small, fair woman. She is considered a good driver. Ha! I see also a tall, dark woman. She is Irish, and sits beside you in the tonneau. The journey is long, but——"

"You said that before," Kathie put in mischievously.

"Now did I?" Leila beamed more broadly.

"Never mind the rest of that fortune. I need my hand." Marjorie caught Leila around the waist and hugged her with vigor.

They had reached the garage now and were standing near the doorway waiting for Vera and the roadster.

"You and Vera are going to Sanford with me, you darling!" was the delighted lieutenant's cry. "It will be the greatest lark imaginable—to go home in the roadster. How I wish Robin and Kathie could go, too."

"Sorry," Kathie's one word of regret spoke volumes.

"So am I," echoed Robin. "I'm going home with Marjorie at Christmas if I can. I know you girls will have a gorgeous time."

As the five took places in the car they talked of the trip Leila had planned to Sanford and of the engagements they had made previous to Wednesday. On Monday evening Miss Remson and the five post graduates were to be entertained at dinner by President and Mrs. Matthews. Tuesday afternoon and evening were to be spent at Hamilton Arms. What with luncheon at Baretti's on Monday at one o'clock and luncheon the next day at the Lotus their time was well filled.

While the roadster was traveling the stretch of highway which formed a complete southern boundary of the college campus the chums again happened upon Miss Monroe. To see her was to admire her beauty afresh without inquiring into her failings. The sleeveless frock she wore, a delicate French creation of pale green silk and filmy white net, served to enhance the astonishing whiteness of her throat, shoulders and arms. Under the pale green lining of a white parasol which she held between herself and the too-ardent sun, her eyes shone forth, deeply mysteriously green. There was artistry in the rather simple waving and coiffing of her spun gold hair. White silk stockings and white suede slippers completed a costume which made her appear so charmingly lovely the chums found themselves regretting her lack of sociability.

"It is too bad not to ask her to go with us," Marjorie said in a low tone to Leila. "I imagine she is out for a walk today because she is lonely."

"Let us see. I will be the first to disregard my own advice." Leila rose to the occasion wholly to please Marjorie.

"Oh, Leila, I'd rather you———"

Leila leaned forward and said: "Stop the wagon, Midget." She flashed Marjorie a smile of utter good humor. "Don't worry, Beauty. I shall not groan with broken bones."

Miss Monroe was strolling along the time-worn stone walk of the college which lay between the highway and the campus wall. On the other side of the highway was only a footpath. Her attention fixed on the opposite side of the highway she had not noted the stopping of the roadster. She turned her eyes ahead only when she had come up within a few feet of it. Her face darkened with annoyance. She half turned as though about to bolt in an opposite direction. Then she tossed her blonde head and advanced along the walk.

"Good afternoon, Miss Monroe," Leila leaned out of the car. "We're off for a ride and dinner at Orchard Inn. Won't you come with us?" Leila conscientiously endeavored to put persuasive friendliness into the invitation.

"No." Miss Monroe stopped short and shook a decisive head. "I don't care in the least for that sort of treat. Thank you." A chilly smile flickered only to die on her lips.

"We're going to have luncheon at Baretti's on Monday——" Marjorie spoke the rest of the invitation into the air. Miss Monroe had gone on, apparently without having heard it.

"I have no patience with that girl!" Vera broke out indignantly as the discourteous student continued to put distance between herself and the carload of girls. In her vexation Vera allowed the car to stand for an instant.

"Uh-h-h!" Leila was cautiously going over her arms, shoulders and hands for broken bones. "Keep your temper, Midget. Your Irish friend is still alive. So is Beauty; who thinks she is talking to someone, and finds she has been talking to the wind."

"Better luck another day. I decline to abandon the field of honor," Marjorie said with cheerful undauntedness. "I believe the fairy-tale princess has been enchanted by a wicked wizard and is under a magic spell. Some day I'm going to break the spell."

CHAPTER XVII.
"BLONDIE"

Doris Monroe glanced in contemptuous fashion at the roadster when, a moment or two later, it sped past her on the highway. Far from being appreciative of the helpful spirit which had lived in spite of the rebuff she had given the Travelers, she felt instead that she had an actual grievance against them. She had chosen to take offense at the time of the evening and the informality which had attended their call on her. For this she had labeled them as ill-bred; *gauche*; stupid. She had seen plenty of American girls in England and on the Continent. She thought she detested them. In reality she did not. Her trouble began with herself. She had always been so completely wrapped up in herself that she now had no interest in any other girl of her own age. Secure in her unusual beauty she lived only to please Doris Monroe. Marjorie's whimsy concerning Doris as an enchanted princess under the spell of a wicked wizard was nearer truth than fancy. Self was a powerful wizard likely to keep the spoiled girl in bondage indefinitely.

Her mother had died when she was five years old. Her father, an American, of English descent, had won considerable prestige as an explorer. London or Paris was home to him, however, when he returned to civilization from his long expeditions into the Tropics. When at home he had paid a fair amount of attention to the bringing up and educating of his daughter. When on a trip he had left her in the care of a governess or at a private school for girls. She had had a succession of governesses. She had attended both English and French Schools. Of college, particularly college in the United States, she knew nothing. The fact that her father had suddenly decided to ship her to Hamilton College before going on the Amazon expedition was still a sore matter with her.

She had arrived on the campus in much the same spirit as a stirred-up porcupine, ready to launch a shower of quills at the first person who chanced to offend her. She was bitterly angry with her father for sending her to college and she transferred that anger to Hamilton as soon as she arrived at Wayland Hall. She despised her room, the campus, Miss Remson—most of all she detested the five P. G.'s who were altogether too ready to become friendly.

Doris was not looking forward to the opening of the college as a relief for loneliness. All her short life she had been so well satisfied with herself for company that she had rarely made acquaintance with other girls. Of the joys of having a chum she knew nothing. While she considered the campus "a ghastly dull spot" she had no happy anticipations of the "mobs" of girls which she dreaded to see invade it.

She was thinking of this not far distant calamity, which she could not avoid, as she walked sulkily along the highway wondering what to do that afternoon by way of amusement. Those stupid girls had acted as though she were a beggar to whom they were trying to be kind. Her red lips curved scornfully at thought of their stupidity. She decided she would take a taxicab into the town of Hamilton. She hoped she would meet "the cheeky things" on the way. It would prove to them that she could go driving if she chose. What to do in Hamilton she did not know. Go to a tea shop for an ice, perhaps.

She presently hailed a taxicab returning from a trip on the campus, an only, but lovely occupant. Half way to town she passed a white roadster, which, though conspicuous, compelled her admiration. It was driven by Leslie Cairns, to whom Doris paid not the slightest attention. Leslie, on the contrary, stared hard at Doris. During the week she had now been in Hamilton she had seen Doris twice; once at the Lotus; once near the campus.

The defeat of her unscrupulous plan to prevent Marjorie Dean and Robin Page from obtaining the site they desired for the dormitory they purposed to build had not discouraged Leslie Cairns. She owned property next to the dormitory site presented by Miss Hamilton she had reflected, with her strange hobgoblin smile. Through Lola Ester, who had been graduated in the same class with Marjorie, she had learned that Marjorie and Robin were to return to Hamilton during the summer in the interest of the proposed dormitory. Leslie had decided immediately that she, also, would return, and had laid plans accordingly.

In itself the idea of building a garage on her land after it had been cleared of the row of old houses had not specially interested Leslie. She had used the garage prospect merely as an excuse for buying the property away from the girls she disliked. Now she had a fresh incentive to proceed with it. It would give her untold opportunity to keep in touch with the undertaking of which Marjorie Dean was the strongest power. Further, she would hear the news of the college; possibly meet a few students who might amuse her.

If Leslie Cairns had been graduated from Hamilton College, instead of having been expelled from it she would have probably lost all interest in it. Her contrary disposition caused her to value, too late, that which she had irretrievably lost by her own unworthiness. Not for worlds would she have confessed that she cared a button about the forfeited diploma. Nevertheless, she cared. The diploma would have meant her father's proud favor. It was galling to her to know that she had been the one to close the gates of Hamilton College against herself. That particular bitter reflection boosted her interest in Hamilton as nothing else could have done. It also strengthened an ignoble desire toward any malicious mischief which her willing hand might find to do.

The day before leaving Newport she had bought the smart white roadster which she was now driving and had ordered it to be driven to the town of Hamilton. It had not arrived until a week later and she had been obliged either to hire a car temporarily or walk. She had been driving the hired car on the Sunday evening when she had passed Vera's roadster on Hamilton Highway.

Sight of Leslie Cairns' uncomely face, suddenly appearing out of the darkness, had surprised, but not dismayed, Marjorie. Leila had been concerned by it to the extent of exclaiming sarcastically: "Now why was I not at the station to meet her?" None of the other three girls had glimpsed her in that instant of betraying light. It was not until the quintette were crossing the campus to the Hall from the garage that Leila told them the news. Girl-like they had exclaimed over it. With the exception of Leila they had spoken of Leslie Cairns far more kindly than she deserved. Leila was, what she liked to call herself, "a good Irish hater." She and Leslie had entered Hamilton College in the same autumn. She had often said candidly to Marjorie and her chums that she detested Leslie more thoroughly than any other girl she had ever known.

Leila had joined the fight for democracy at Hamilton, which Marjorie and her Sanford friends had made during their freshman year, chiefly because she enjoyed thwarting Leslie Cairns and the other San Soucians. Later, when she had come to know and understand Marjorie's fine nature, her own really great soul responded to it. She had fought then for democracy because she loved Marjorie and believed in fair play. She continued, however, to hold and be proud of her animosity toward Leslie Cairns.

The old saying: "There's many a true word spoken in jest" seemed on the way to be proven so far as Doris Monroe and Leslie Cairns were concerned. Leila's satirical opinion of the "fine time" the two might spend together because of their common lack of courtesy was on the way to come to pass. Leslie had decided in the moment when her car passed the taxicab holding Doris that she wished to meet "Blondie," as she mentally named the other girl.

Leslie's wish became her law whenever she could encompass it. She turned the white roadster about as soon as she could and sent it speeding in the direction taken by the station taxicab. She caught sight of the dark blue taxi as she whizzed around a curve with reckless speed. That the road chanced to be clear was her good fortune. She smiled to herself, muttering: "No more of that kind of business. I'll be apt to let myself in for trouble. But I had to pick up that taxi."

With the blue taxicab now in sight and her car close behind it Leslie began to speculate on Doris' destination. "I'll say she's bound for eats; either at the Lotus, or the Ivy."

"The Ivy it is?" she surmised triumphantly as the taxicab continued on down Herndon Avenue and up Linden Avenue. "I'll watch her into the Ivy; then I think I'll stroll in there, too. My guess—she's on the campus, stuffing for her entrance exams. She's certainly not visiting Remson or any other of the campus aggregation of frumps. I think it's my duty to get acquainted with Blondie."

CHAPTER XVIII.
A CONGENIAL PAIR

A satiric smile still lingered at the comers of Leslie Cairn's unlovely mouth as she entered the Ivy in her careless, near-slouching manner. The irregular plainness of her features was more pronounced than usual by reason of the stunning afternoon frock she wore of expensive creamy buff material. Unlike the severe style of sports clothes she affected it had the feminine lure of soft folds and exquisite creamy buff Persian embroidery. Her full white throat rose gracefully from the round open neck. The very short sleeves would have shown a pair of well-rounded arms had she not worn long gloves to match her gown. Her French-heeled slippers of the same material as her gown and the silk embroidered hosiery of palest buff completed her "foolish rig" as she slangily dubbed it. She was without a hat and her hair had been waved and artistically dressed.

Doris had already settled herself at a side table in the tea room and was perusing the menu with an air of boredom. Leslie, advancing toward the other girl, decided that "Blondie" was as pretty as Bean, if not prettier. She saw triumphs ahead of the supposed freshie if she did not "flunk her exams." Already a daring plan had entered her scheming brain.

As she dropped casually into the place at table directly opposite Doris the latter raised her eyes from the menu card. Very deliberately the strange greenish eyes took stock of Leslie. Leslie returned the survey with one equally prolonged. The two girls forgot etiquette and stared at each other like two curious children. Such they were; two children of impulse, both spoiled by neglect and indulgence.

"Pardon me," Leslie broke the spell in the smoothest of tones. "I am sure I have met you before. Let me think." She pretended to ponder. "Wasn't it at the fancy dress ball Mrs. Russell Fennimore gave at her town house last March? It was a rather jolly affair. What?"

"No." The monosyllable was decided. Leslie's imported gown commanded a certain respect from Doris. "I am not yet in society," she volunteered, not without interest. "I've not been presented at Court."

"Oh-h!" Up went Leslie's shaggy eye-brows. "You are English," she placed flattering stress on the last word. "Isn't that ripping?"

"No, I'm not English." Doris sighed. "I wish I were. I'm of English descent, though." She brightened a little.

"So am I," glibly asserted Leslie, "but I'd rather live in America than in England. I've been across the pond a dozen times."

"I prefer either England or France to the United States," Doris said somewhat stiffly. "Paris is my favorite of all cities."

"It's not bad." Leslie turned faintly patronizing. "Give me New York above them all. Don't you like New York? What."

"I don't know it," Doris was forced to admit. She colored faintly. Leslie's impassive features and nonchalant air of self-possession were very disturbing to her. In the face of them she found it hard to keep up an indifferent pose. She experienced a contrary desire to talk to Leslie and find out who she was. Since her advent on the campus she had seen no one else she had come nearer to approving. Still she had no intention of allowing this beautifully dressed, ugly stranger to patronize her.

"You aren't really a bit English," she now said sweetly to Leslie. "I mean in the way you talk. You use a few common English words and phrases in the English way; but they sound American."

Leslie's brows began to draw together as Doris launched this "nervy" criticism. All of a sudden her face cleared. She treated Doris to one of her odd silent laughs. Here was a girl after her own heart. "Blondie" evidently had no more compunction than she about hurting another person's feelings. She was keen-witted enough to see that she must travel a wary road to friendship with her "find." Doris was sufficient unto herself.

"Have you ordered luncheon?" she asked irrelevantly, ignoring Doris' unflattering opinion. "The chicken a la king is particularly good here." Leslie picked up a menu card and busied herself with it.

"Thank you. I believe I *will* order it." Doris waited for Leslie to say something else.

Leslie had nothing to say. She beckoned to a waitress and proceeded to carry on a wise consultation with her concerning the items on the menu. Doris began to feel ill at ease. Her brief exchange of talk with Leslie had filled her with a sudden desire to continue the conversation.

The waitress, having written down Leslie's order, turned inquiringly to Doris.

"Chicken a la king," Doris began confidently, without looking at the menu, "and——" she glanced at Leslie. Leslie had taken a small white kid note book from a strap purse she carried and was industriously making notes in it with a tiny white pencil.

"Why don't you duplicate my order?" Leslie was not too busy to miss Doris' hesitating tone. "I know what's good to eat here."

"I will, thank you." Again Doris found herself answering Leslie with almost meek politeness.

"That's good." Leslie closed the little book, put it and the pencil in the purse and straightened her shoulders in a faithful imitation of her father. Believing that Doris would eventually prove useful to her she cleverly resolved to treat "Blondie" as her father might have treated a business subordinate who was his social equal.

While waiting for the luncheon to be served the two reached slightly better terms. Doris told Leslie her name, her father's name and a little concerning her life abroad. Leslie introduced herself by name, but gave Doris no other information save that her father was a millionaire financier. Leslie was deliberating as to how much of her Hamilton history she should tell Doris. If she expected to become friendly with "Blondie" she must acquaint her with a glossed over account of her expulsion from college. Sooner or later Doris would be sure to hear an echo of it on the campus.

"How do you like Wayland Hall?" Leslie inquired, when, in the course of conversation Doris remarked her residence there.

"I don't like it at all," Doris shrugged her dislike.

"It's the best house on the campus. I lived there for almost four years. I ought to know." Leslie came out boldly with the information.

"You did!" Doris laid down her salad fork and surveyed Leslie with genuine astonishment. "Then you were graduated from Hamilton College. Were you graduated last June?"

"No," Leslie gained dramatic effect by a slow, pensive shake of the head. Her loose-lipped mouth tightened into pretended regret. "I was preparing to be graduated a year ago last June. A senior, supposed to be my dear friend, started a hazing story about me and sixteen other girls. We were all members of a very exclusive club. We asked the girl who made the trouble for us to resign from our club. She had circulated untrue stories about us on the campus. For pure spite she wrote a letter to Prexy Matthews, claiming that we hazed a junior on a certain winter night.

"You see," Leslie continued with elaborate earnestness, "on St. Valentine's night the juniors always give a masquerade ball in the gym. Before the dance the maskers walk around on the campus and kid one another and any one else who happens to cross the campus without a mask. Even the faculty are fair game for kidding. Some of us started to have a little fun with a prig of a junior by the name of Dean. We bothered her a trifle; nothing to speak of. We got away with it O. K., but we had a traitor in our own crowd. She told the biggest gossip on the campus about it. We held a club meeting, called her down and asked for her resignation. Then she put Prexy on our trail. We were all expelled from college only a few weeks before we would have been graduated. I might have saved myself—I don't know." Leslie put on a self-sacrificing air.

Doris' earlier indifference had completely vanished with the knowledge that Leslie had been a student at Hamilton. Her interest increased as Leslie continued her narrative.

"If any such trouble had happened to me I'd never wish to see Hamilton College again," was Doris' view of the matter. "Most girls are so deceitful. I wouldn't go to the pains to be. I think it's snaky to be deceitful, even in little things."

"Yes, isn't it?" Leslie cheerfully concurred. "I'm glad you feel so about it. It is hard to find a really sincere girl whom one can trust."

Doris was not specially impressed by Leslie's remarks. Under her fairy-tale princess exterior she possessed a stolid side of character which did not respond to flattery. She knew she was beautiful. She did not need the assurance from others. She believed herself not deceitful. Leslie's opinion of her sincerity did not matter.

"There's a Miss Dean at Wayland Hall now," Doris remarked, her interest still hovering over Leslie's story of the hazing.

"That is the one," Leslie said impressively. "I knew she was somewhere on the campus. I supposed she would be at Wayland Hall. All I have to say of her is—well——" Leslie made an effective pause. "I'd prefer to say nothing," she ended with a sigh.

"I have met her, and the girls she goes with. One of them is of the faculty; four are post graduates. I do not like any of them," Doris announced with flat finality. "I *detest* Miss Remson."

A crafty gleam appeared in Leslie's small dark eyes. Here was better luck than she had hoped for. "I understand the way you feel," she nodded with deceitful sympathy. "I had three years at the Hall with Miss Dean and her bunch. It was more than enough for me. As for Remson——" Leslie spread her hands in a deprecatory gesture—"She's hopeless."

"I can't endure her," Doris agreed with more energy of tone than she had previously used. "She imagines herself of such importance. She is merely an upper servant." The girl's short upper lip lifted in scorn.

Miss Remson had bitterly offended Doris by paying no attention to her after she had snubbed the five Travelers. The wise little manager had decided to let the supercilious young woman work out her own salvation. She spoke courteously to Doris when she chanced to encounter her about the house, but not one word of pleasantry did she offer. Long experience with girl nature had taught her the value of such a course in a case where false pride, instead of good breeding dominated.

"Think of me!" Leslie leaned confidentially forward toward Doris. "I stood her and that baby-booby bunch of Be—er—Miss Dean's friends for years. Of course I had a dandy pal. That helped a whole lot. Then the Sans, our club gang, were a zippy bunch. We all had cars at Hamilton. Some of the girls had two chug wagons apiece. Money was no object. There were scads of coin behind our gang. All the Sans' governors were millionaires, most of 'em multi-millionaires, hitting the financial high spots."

Stung by Doris' criticism of her imitation of an English drawl Leslie had wisely dropped it. Instead, she began flavoring her remarks with slang by way of impressing her companion. Leslie had shrewdly appraised Doris during the luncheon. She now believed that she understood "Blondie" and would be able to manage her.

"I wanted my maid to come here with me, but my father wouldn't let me have her," pouted Doris. "Celeste would have been better company than a lot of stupid students."

Leslie forgot the rôle she had essayed to play of light good humor. Her famous scowl, heavy and disfiguring showed itself. Blondie was not impressed by her slang, her troubles or her money. "You don't want a maid at college," she scoffed gruffly. "I wouldn't be bothered with one, even coming here from Newport. I sent my maid on a vacation."

"I wish Celeste were with me," Doris obstinately repeated. As if determined to be contrary she continued. "There's one girl at the Hall that I'd not call baby-booby. She is really distingué. I don't recall her name. She said to me that she was born in Ireland and——"

"Leila Harper!" was Leslie's interrupting exclamation. "She is clever as a wizard, and a terror. She's crazy about Miss Dean and her gang. Look out for her. I don't care to gossip, but perhaps I'd better tell you some things about that crowd. You ought to know them. After luncheon why not take a spin with me in my car? Maybe you've seen it. It's white, and a dream. I'd love to have you come along."

Leslie had forced back her rising irritation and turned pleasant again.

"Thank you, but——" Doris hesitated. She regarded Leslie with a thoughtful, innocent air which was a mask she assumed. Behind it she studied Leslie's ugly, almost grotesque features and the expensive luxury of her costume. Self, the little inner deity Doris worshipped, bade her accept the invitation and enjoy the ride. If she did not approve afterward of Leslie it would be easy enough to snub her roundly. "I'll come with you. It's no end kind in you to ask me," she accepted without enthusiasm.

"So glad to have you." Leslie managed to keep sarcastic inflection out of her reply. She was already beginning to discover that Blondie was "certainly a selfish proposition." Still, try as she might where could she have found another girl so well suited to her purpose?

"Great work," she congratulated herself as the two girls emerged from the Ivy to where the white car stood in all its creamy, glittering glory. "Blondie is down on Remson, can't stand Bean and the Bean stalks and she lives at Wayland Hall. She knows me and we're going to be chummy. It's as good as a private wire between me and the Hall. Can you beat it?"

CHAPTER XIX.
GENTLEMAN GUS

"Marjorie Dean-n! Oo-oo; oo-oo! Mar-r-jo-r-ie D-e-an!"

Marjorie turned sharply as the long resonant call was borne to her ears on the crisp fall air. Speeding toward her across the campus came a tall girl, hands cupped to her lips. She was running with a certain individual, energetic swing of body which Marjorie recognized as belonging to but one student at Hamilton. Sight of her brought a sunny smile to Marjorie's somewhat serious face.

"Gussie Forbes," she cried, "are you really here at last. She held out both hands to the tall handsome sophomore whose own face was radiant.

"I am, but I'm surprised to think that I ever reached here." Gussie grasped the welcoming hands and shook them with vigor. "I've been at Wayland Hall about fifteen minutes. I asked where you were, first thing. Miss Remson said she thought you were somewhere on the campus, so out I hustled to try to find you."

"Faithful Gussie. What can I do to reward such devotion?" laughed Marjorie.

"Come back to the Hall with me and be the feature of a rejoicing bow-wow in Flossie's and my room," came the prompt return. "We're all simply perishing to see you and the rest of the Sanfordites. Is Miss Lynde back? I never dare call her Ronny, though I think she's a perfect dear." Gussie linked an arm in one of Marjorie's and began towing her gently toward the Hall.

"Ronny's here. She stopped at Sanford for us on her way from California. Jerry, Lucy, Ronny and I came back together. Muriel's not coming back this year."

"Oh, dear!" wailed Gussie. "That's bad news. Muriel is such a lot of fun. I only knew her well toward the last of the college year, but we were getting quite chummy."

"We're all sorry Muriel isn't with us." Marjorie's face fell at the remembrance. "We're going to miss her dreadfully. We tried to coax her to come with us, but she said 'no' and wouldn't give a reason for saying it. She's been very mysterious about it."

"Haven't you the least idea of why she isn't coming back?" questioned Gussie curiously.

"No. She insists that she isn't engaged to be married. That would be her strongest reason for not coming back."

"Aggravating old goose," was Gussie's fond opinion of Muriel. "Look out she isn't simply kidding you. I'll bet she's engaged."

"You asked for Ronny. There she is now on the steps." Marjorie waved a gay signal to Veronica Lynde, who answered it in kind.

"She sent me a set of ducky postcards from Lower California this summer. I was so surprised. I never thought she'd do that." Gussie spoke humbly.

"You've a bad case of too much respect for Ronny," laughed Marjorie. "If she discovers it she will give you a good shaking."

"I wish she would," sighed Gussie. "I'd feel more at home with her afterward. I behaved like a savage to you last year. I'm sure Miss Lynde hasn't forgiven me for that. She was pleasant with me after I turned civilized, but never friendly."

A smile dimpled the corners of Marjorie's mouth. "It's all right," she cheered downcast Gussie. "You're friends with Ronny, only you didn't know it. She loathes writing letters, or even postcards. You've had the sign and seal of her friendship."

"Ha-a-a-a! Tell you that's fine news," Gussie instantly brightened.

As the two girls neared Ronny she came down the steps and advanced to meet them. "So glad to see you again." She greeted Augusta with a warmth which completely assured the doubting sophomore of her friendliness.

"And what have *you* been doing, Miss M. M. Dean?" she humorously interrogated Marjorie.

"I'd started for Silverton Hall to see Robin and Phil. Phil has a great idea she wants to tell Robin and me about. Now the great idea will have to wait. I'm going to a pow-wow in Gussie's room."

"No one invited me to a pow-wow." Ronny turned reproachful eyes on Gussie. "I enjoy pow-wows far more than Marjorie does."

"I invite you to one this minute. Excuse my seeming neglect. I've been at the Hall just long enough to set down my luggage and start out to find Marjorie. Double delighted to find your Highness, too." Gussie made Ronny an exaggerated, respectful bow. Now sure of Ronny's approval she entered blithely into the spirit of Veronica's teasing remarks.

"Will you ask Jerry and Lucy to come and meet the gang in my room?" Gussie was in a pleasant flutter of excitement as the trio reached the second floor of the Hall. "Flossie went for Leila and Vera. They're probably at the party now."

"I'll answer for Jerry, and trot her to the pow-wow directly," Marjorie promised.

"Lucy's still in our room. I think. You may expect us." Ronny returned Gussie's salute with one equally extravagant and disappeared into her room.

"She's a perfect love! I won't need that shaking after all," Gussie confided to Marjorie with sparkling eyes as the two separated briefly.

Marjorie hurried lightly down the hall and opened the door of Room 15. "Hello, Jeremiah," she greeted; "Gussie Forbes is back. We're invited to a pow-wow in her room this very moment."

"Well, well, well; you don't mean it." Jerry Macy looked up with an incredulous grin from the letter she was writing.

"Yes, I do mean it." Marjorie pounced upon Jerry and tried to pull her up from her chair. Jerry grinningly braced herself and remained firm.

"You can't do it, Marvelous Manager. I'm someone you can't manage. So Gentleman Gus is going to have a pow-wow! Shall Jeremiah attend it, or finish her letter? Which? What?" Jerry had applied the nickname "Gentleman Gus," to Augusta Forbes because of the number of male rôles the tall, broad-shouldered sophomore had played in campus shows during her freshman year.

"You'll attend it," was Marjorie's threatening prediction as she began a fresh onslaught upon her apparently stationary chum. "If I can't haul you up from that chair I'll go for reinforcements. Then we'll see what'll happen."

"Just see what's happened already." Jerry sprang up from the chair. "Why, Bean, respected Bean, excuse me. I nearly tipped you over, didn't I?" she innocently apologized as she bumped smartly against her roommate.

"Oh, never mind. You don't know any better," Marjorie made charitable allowance as she tucked her arm in Jerry's and moved resolutely toward the door.

In front of the closed door of Gussie's room Marjorie smiled and raised a finger. Inside a merry babel of fresh young voices told them the pow-wow was in full swing. Marjorie tapped lightly on the door. No one answering, she turned the knob and she and Jerry entered the room. Ronny, Lucy, Leila and Vera formed a group around which the five sophomore chums known to their friends as the Bertramites had gathered.

At sight of Marjorie and Jerry a mild shout went up from the assembled nine. Gussie made a jubilant dash from the group to receive them.

"For goodness sake, girls, moderate your whoops of joy," cautioned Flossie Hart when she could make herself heard above the commotion. "The Hall is full of young and timid freshies. This warning isn't meant for you P. G.'s," she laughingly excepted. "Only the Bertramites are included in it."

"A pow-wow is a pow-wow. I'm surprised at you, Floss," reproved Calista Wilmot with a giggle.

"Remember eats are necessary at a pow-wow. Trot out whatever you happen to have in your suitcases that's eatable," Gussie ordered. "I've a five-pound box of chocolate nuts. Next? That means Floss, Calista, Charlotte and Anna. The rest of you are company and have to be entertained."

Gussie cleared the center table with one or two energetic sweeps of the arm. Her chums began a prompt diving into bags and suitcases for their contributions to the feast. Calista produced a pasteboard box of macaroons, Flossie one of salted almonds, Anna a sweet grass basket of stuffed dates and Charlotte Robbins a box of home-made maple and chocolate fudge and a large jar of tiny sour pickles.

"There." Gussie arranged the toothsome array of delicacies on the table to her satisfaction. "Here's to our noble P. G.'s," she proposed, flourishing an arm. "Long may they wave. Hurrah, hurrah, hurrah!"

The five Bertramites came out lustily on the hurrahing. The room rang with their gleeful shouts.

The echoes of them had hardly died out before the six guests were returning the compliment quite as vociferously. They continued to make plenty of pleasant noise as they sampled the sweets and rushed from one topic of girl interest to another.

"Someone is rapping on the door." Leila's quick ears were the first to catch the sound.

"I'll go." Gussie hurried to the door, a pickle in one hand, a square of maple fudge in the other. She transferred the pickle to the fudge hand and opened the door.

"Why, Miss Remson!" Her eyes widened in surprise. "Come in. We're having a jollification. You are just in time for it."

"Glad to join in the fun." The manager's tones were utterly friendly. "I'm the bearer of wet-blanket news, though. Miss Monroe, next door to this room, has just complained of the noise going on here. She has an examination in mathematics tomorrow and insists upon quiet so that she can study. I'm sorry, children." A good-humored smile overspread her face. "You'll have to try to play more quietly."

"Why, the idea! We haven't been here an hour yet, and it's so early in the afternoon!" Gussie burst forth half resentfully. "Pardon me, Miss Remson. I don't mean that for you. I mean it for fussy Miss Monroe, whoever she may be. Talk about pure freshie nerve!" Gussie's eyes traveled the group of now silent students for sympathy. She found it in the common expression of blank, half-sheepish surprise written large on her friends' faces.

"Miss Monroe isn't a freshman, Augusta," the manager corrected gently. "She is trying the examinations this week which will admit her to the sophomore class. I explained to her that you and Miss Hart were sophomores, hoping she might make allowance."

"A would-be soph, and complaining of the sophs! What a loyal addition to the sophie class she will be," Florence Hart cried sarcastically.

"Not wishing to be too inquisitive, Miss Remson, may I ask if Miss Monroe insisted you should come and tell us what a noisy crowd we were?" Leila inquired smoothly.

"Yes, Leila; she did," the little woman replied in her concise way.

"Now why, I wonder, did she not come and tell us herself?" Leila's tones were silky, but her blue eyes had narrowed.

Miss Remson laughed. "Clever Leila," she regarded the Irish girl with approbation. "I may as well tell you girls frankly. Miss Monroe put it to me as my duty to reprimand you. I hope you won't consider my enforced word of caution in the nature of a reprimand," she ended with the independence of affection.

A chorus of loyal assurances went up which caused her to raise a premonitory hand and incline her head in the direction of the next room. After stopping long enough to eat a square of fudge and two pickles with true schoolgirl appetite she left behind her an ominously quiet crowd of girls.

"A nice reputation you have as a P. G., Jeremiah Macy." Jerry severely addressed herself in the mirror of a dressing table. "Just think"—she turned accusingly toward Lucy Warner—"even Luciferous Warniferous, the Sanford sage, got a hot shot for being too boisterous."

"Don't blame me. Blame the company I keep," chuckled Lucy.

"Luciferous Warniferous couldn't be boisterous if she tried," defended Ronny. "She hasn't said half a dozen words since I led her into this room. I know she hasn't whooped once. Can you whoop, Luciferous? That's what I'd love to know?" Ronny peered owlishly at Lucy.

"Don't give a demonstration of it till we are out on the campus," warned Anna Perry. Her inflection was sarcastic. "It's not safe here."

"I sha'n't give one at any time or at any place," Lucy retorted with great firmness.

"The very idea," scolded Flossie Hart. "Why, we made twice as much noise when we first came to the Hall last year and no one made a fuss."

"I won't stand it." Gussie Forbes shook back her short curls, squared her shoulders and linked her hands behind her back in the attitude her chums knew meant battle. "Can't help it if this Miss Monroe is going to be a soph. She might have known we'd subside. She could have waited a little to see. I won't be mean enough to say I hope she flunks in math. But I'll say she'll flunk in popularity if she can't live and let live."

CHAPTER XX.
BETTER LATE THAN NEVER

That evening in Ronny's room Leila, Vera, Marjorie and Jerry gathered for one of their old-time "Traveler" meetings. The arrival of Ronny's trunks had furnished a treat of Mexican sweets, tempting and varied. There were all sorts of candied tropical fruits, strange toothsome nut pastes and a golden delicious sweet called *dulce*. There were even candied sweet potatoes.

"Get busy and help yourselves," Ronny directed as she placed the large square tin box of confections on the table before her chums. "I've a supply of Mexican candy on hand. I'm going to take this box to *l'enfant angelique*." She smiled as she referred to Gussie Forbes by the title the chums had privately re-named her after her change of heart during her freshman year. "Back in a minute." Ronny flitted from the room burdened with a second square tin box of sweets.

"Gentleman Gus needs a reward of good conduct for keeping her temper this afternoon. She was all ready to turn the pow-wow into a real tomahawking party with one blonde scalp for a trophy," was Jerry's opinion.

"I expected an explosion," Marjorie confessed with a smile; "but none came. Gussie is splendid, I think."

"How perfectly foolish in Miss Monroe to take such a ridiculous stand! I can't help criticizing her for it," Vera said disapprovingly. "In the face of not knowing whether she will pass her exams or not."

"If she flunks in the soph exams, she can still try for freshie estate," Lucy reminded.

"It seems she likes no one but herself," Leila now made dry observation. "We thought in the summer it was only the four of us at the Hall and Kathie who were not to her taste. Now we may banish our sorrow. We are no worse off than the rest of the college."

"Such a relief to my mind," snickered Jerry. During the three or four days that the Sanford group of girls had been back at Hamilton she had seen Doris Monroe half a dozen times and had formed one of her peculiar dislikes to the self-centered young woman. "Behave Jeremiah." She gave one plump wrist a resounding whack. "Remember the stranger; et-cætera; et-cætera."

"But never think about your old friends." A tall girl in a gray sports coat and hat, her charming face alive with laughter, had opened the door on Jerry's curtailed quotation of Hamilton's first tradition.

"Muriel Harding; you rascal of rascals!" Jerry reached the newcomer at a bound. She caught her about the waist and pranced Muriel over the floor in a wild dance which landed both against the opposite wall with force.

"Call off Jeremiah," begged Muriel mirthfully. "She's too rough to belong in polite society. The rest of you aren't much more ladylike," she called out as a determined quartette hemmed her in and attempted to embrace her in a body.

"You deserve rough house tactics," declared Jerry. The happy light in her eyes told another story. The other girls' faces also reflected their pleasure in Muriel's return.

"You mysterious old goose. I can't think of anything to say to you that would be really disrespectful," Marjorie assured the broadly beaming Traveler. "We've missed you dreadfully. I'm so glad you're back."

"So am I. I was fairly sure she wouldn't desert us," Lucy said with a wise nod of her dark head. "She used to make fun of me so much that I learned her tricks. I had an idea all the time that she couldn't stay away from this illustrious crowd."

"How sweet in you all to miss me." Muriel wept a few mock tears of appreciation into her handkerchief. "As for you, Luciferous, *you* know too much." She treated Lucy to a glare of displeasure which broke up in mirth. Lucy's rare, childish giggle invariably sent Muriel into peals of laughter.

In the midst of the hilarity Ronny re-appeared and a fresh burst of welcoming began. Once or twice it occurred to Marjorie that they were making almost as much commotion as had the party of girls in Gussie's room that afternoon. Freshmen occupied the rooms on either side of Ronny and Lucy. They were evidently less fussy than was Miss Monroe.

"Now tell us all about it," Marjorie coaxed when Muriel had been fondly divested of coat and hat and established in the room's most comfy chair.

"All about what?" Muriel pretended wide-eyed innocence.

"You know; just go right ahead and talk," Jerry coolly invited. "No use in asking us questions."

"Um-m-m. Perhaps you are right, my dear Jeremiah," Muriel conceded sweetly. "Well, I thought it would be wonderful to be missed. I knew that neither you, Ronny, nor you, Jeremiah had proper regard for me. I had my doubts about Lucy. I knew Bean was a kindly creature who would at least think she missed me. But I wanted all of you to feel the heart-breaking sadness of not seeing me around and circulating merrily on the campus. So I decided to put you all to the test, and——"

"Fakir," hissed Ronny making a serpentine dive for Muriel's chair and landing on an arm of it. She promptly clapped a hand over Muriel's mouth. "You sha'n't say another word until you promise to tell us the real reason."

Muriel uttered a series of unintelligible remarks behind Ronny's hand. She held up her own right hand finally as a sign of compliance. Ronny reluctantly took away the barrier to speech.

"This is the truth, girls, the whole truth, and nothing but the truth. I almost got myself engaged to be married, but not quite." Muriel's pretty features grew rosy as she made this naive confession. "It was on that account I was so mysterious about coming back. It's Harry Lenox, of course. I may marry him someday." Muriel waved an indefinite hand. "Really, I didn't know what I wanted to do until the last minute. After you girls were gone from Sanford I couldn't bear to be left out of building the dormitory and switching around the campus as a venerable P. G. So here I am. Yours truly." Muriel favored her audience with one of her wide captivating smiles.

"Much ado about nothing," Jerry commented derisively.

"Precisely," beamed Muriel. "Let me return the compliment. 'Shallow brooks babble loudest.'"

"I think Miss Remson said she had half a room left, Muriel," Vera said presently when the excitement attending Muriel's unexpected arrival had abated.

"Oh, glorious! I hadn't dare hope for a vacancy at the Hall. I thought I'd be lucky to get into any campus house. I suppose the Hall will be full of freshies this year."

"Yes. Some of them haven't arrived yet. We are going to do station duty tomorrow. Help Gussie and the Bertramites out with station detail," Marjorie told Muriel.

"I haven't seen Miss Remson yet. The maid let me in. I'll go down stairs now. My bag and suitcase are in the hall." Muriel rose and walked to the door. "Come on, gang, and go with me," she crooked an inviting finger.

Down the stairs trooped the seven girls, Muriel and Marjorie in the lead. They swarmed Miss Remson's tiny office where the manager sat writing. Her surprise at seeing Muriel was no less than that of the girls had been.

"Vera said you had half a room still open," was Muriel's immediate anxious cry. "If I may have it I'll consider myself the luckiest person under the sun."

Miss Remson sat back in her chair and surveyed Muriel with a perplexed frown. "Yes, there is half a room still vacant," she said, her small keen face full of doubt: "half of Miss Monroe's room." Her gaze traveled to Marjorie and rested inquiringly on the latter's concerned features.

"Oh-h-h!" went up in a breath from the enlightened group.

"What's the matter?" Muriel appeared mystified. "Who's Miss Monroe?" Repetition of the name jogged memory. "Oh, yes; I remember. She's the pretty girl you told me about; the fairy-tale princess; beautiful but icy; et-cætera, et-cætera; as our esteemed roughneck, Jer—. Excuse me. I mean our valued friend Jerry Macy loves to say."

Far from being dismayed at the prospect of an uncongenial roommate Muriel accepted the situation with her usual buoyant spirit. "What's the use in worrying?" she demanded after she had asked numerous questions about her prospective roommate and received nothing but the kindest information her friends could truthfully give. "I know you girls are trying to live up to tradition. I can guess a good deal between the lines about my new roommate."

"Then you are quite sure you wish to make the arrangement, Muriel?" anxiously asked Miss Remson.

"Sure as can be," Muriel flippantly asserted. "I choose to spend my declining P. G. years at the Hall. Shall I turn down such a chance to flourish in the bosom of my friends?"

"You may have my half of Jerry's and my room, Muriel," Marjorie made sudden astounding offer. "I'll room with Miss Monroe instead of you." Marjorie was not sanguine of Muriel's proposed venture. She knew that Muriel and Jerry would be happy together. She was afraid impulsive high-strung Muriel might soon find herself in difficulties. She did not anticipate any smoother sailing for herself. She had reflected before making the offer so characteristic of her unselfish soul that companionship with the strange, unfriendly girl might bring Miss Monroe into a better understanding of Hamilton College.

"Nope." Muriel shook a smiling head. "I'm going to choose the enchanted iceberg for a roommate and see what happens. Are you modest enough to believe that Jeremiah would allow me to supplant you as a roommate? Thank you a million times just the same."

"That's the way to talk. I never credited you with such reasoning power as you have just displayed, my dear Miss Harding." Jerry smiled fatuously upon Muriel then transferred her smiles to Marjorie. "You don't seem to have the least inkling of my deep regard for you. Bean," she reproved.

"You see the way things are?" Marjorie turned to Miss Remson with a laughing gesture.

"Yes, I see." The manager rose from her desk. "Pardon me, children. I had best go upstairs and notify Miss Monroe that her roommate has arrived."

"Tell her she may expect me," giggled Muriel. "You needn't say much about me. I'll astonish her by walking in on her presently with a special P. G. swagger. Nothing succeeds like nerve, you know." Muriel's velvety brown eyes were dancing with mischief.

"I'll back you to win," were Jerry's encouraging words. "You have almost as much nerve as I have; perhaps more."

"I wish I could believe you." Muriel was blandly regretful.

"What a waste of good health to worry over that one, Beauty!" Leila pointed derisively at Muriel.

"I should say so," Ronny agreed with teasing stress. "I'm sorry for the enchanted iceberg."

Marjorie listened and laughed at the exchange of repartee. At the same time she wondered, if, after all, Muriel Harding might not prove to be the best possible roommate for the lovely, ungracious fairy-tale princess.

CHAPTER XXI.
"GOOD HUNTING"

Warned by her chums that her pretty roommate was more than likely to prove frosty, Muriel went to Room 22, armed with her usual light-hearted insouciance, the best weapon she could have had in the circumstances. Far from being cast down by the chilly environment Doris's haughty manner merely appealed to her keen sense of the ridiculous. She gaily named her the Ice Queen and their room the ice chest. "If I stayed in the ice chest too long I might catch cold," she roguishly informed her chums, "but I'm never there more than five minutes at a time except to sleep."

With the filling up of the campus houses with students and the formal opening of Hamilton College the Travelers found their work cut out for them. They spent countless hours in station duty, welcoming arriving freshmen. Feeling their responsibility as post graduates they tried earnestly to promote a spirit of sociability on the campus. These self-imposed duties, besides the effort to keep in touch with their personal campus friends, kept them constantly occupied.

The very reliable, conscientious firm of Page and Dean had the serious duty before them of looking out for the students who had formerly lived in the now demolished houses of the dormitory site. The tenants of the houses in the block which Leslie Cairns had bought had been ordered out of them directly after Commencement. The dingy row of dwellings still stood, awaiting their chagrined owner's pleasure. For a time Leslie had lost interest in the garage idea and had regarded her ill-gotten purchase as an elephant on her hands. Later, she had moodily resolved, because she had nothing else to busy her, to go on with her original plan in the hope of being able, eventually, to even what she considered as a "score" with Marjorie Dean.

After painstaking inquiry and investigation Marjorie and Robin had finally found good boarding places in the town of Hamilton for the seventy-two students who could not afford campus rates. The zealous promoters had also arranged with an Italian, who had recently begun operating a three-bus line between Hamilton and West Hamilton to carry the students to the campus every morning on special trip. More, their old friend Baretti had offered to serve such students with sandwiches and tea, coffee or milk whenever their free hours from recitations should permit them to come to the restaurant. The devoted friend of Page and Dean, the warm-hearted Italian had named a small price for the service. He had been an almost avid supporter of the Travelers' plans and had often hinted that "someday" he would give the "dorm" a nice present.

"Positively, Robin Page," Marjorie declared fervently one soft fall afternoon as the two girls left the dormitory site after a consultation with Peter Graham, "things are simply skimming along. Everything good seems to be gravitating straight toward us. Thanks to Miss Susanna and Jonas the site is clear now and ready for the building. It wouldn't have been cleared before Christmas if they hadn't given us that splendid early start. And where could we find another builder like Mr. Graham? We couldn't; I'm sure."

"Blessing number two," counted Robin, laughing. "We might as well rank Guiseppe Baretti as number three. Think of what he's done for us!"

"I'm thinking," Marjorie nodded. "Then that bus line started up like magic. Just what we needed, when we needed it! And the boarding houses for the off campus girls are fine. Now that they are so beautifully settled we can begin to pick up life on the campus. The freshies this year seem a dandy set of girls."

"So Phil says. She's not crazy over the sophs, though. She says she thinks they are chesty. Not Gussie Forbes and her crowd. Phil likes Gussie. She says there is a lack of college spirit among the others. She hasn't discovered why as yet." Robin looked thoughtful. "I dare say Gussie knows. She is such a live wire."

"I must have a talk with her. Oh, gracious!" Marjorie sighed audibly. "I have so much to do I hardly know what to tackle first. I can't start chemistry again for at least another week. That and French poetry are all I shall undertake this semester."

"I'm going to send for my car," Robin announced with sudden irrelevancy. "I've wasted time waiting for taxis to and from town. We really need my roadster."

"I'd like to have a car here this year," Marjorie admitted honestly. "This is a great secret, Robin. I haven't told another person: General gave me a choice before I came back here between having a car and the money it would cost. I—I took the money. We need it for the dormitory. I know we are welcome to use as much of Ronny's money as we like, but the self-respecting way is to raise it by earning it, or by self-denial."

"You old dear!" Robin patted Marjorie's arm. "You've taught all of us the self-denying way. I spent scads of money when first I came to Hamilton. Now I've turned positively stingy in my old age. I might as well have my car here as home. No one uses it there. I have an excuse for what the up-keep will cost."

Robin was full of her plan to send home for her car. She began to calculate, as the two entered the campus and lingered there for a brief talk, on the saving of time it would mean as against the cost of up-keep. While the absorbed promoters stood talking together a group of half a dozen sophomores passed them. The sophs greeted the two girls' pleasant salutation with a kind of admiring eagerness. Six pairs of bright eyes rested longest on Marjorie, however. One of the girls made a low-voiced remark to the others. There was a concerted shaking of heads as the group passed on.

They had not gone on far when Marjorie said good-bye to Robin and turned her face in the direction of Wayland Hall. The lively murmur of voices close behind her caused her to wheel suddenly. In the next instant a smiling band had surrounded her.

"Oh, Miss Dean, we've something special to ask you," began the leader of the group, a small blue-eyed girl with a round rosy face and deep dimples. "You know the sophs have their election next week. Gussie Forbes is our candidate for president. We want to get up an election parade for her; a regular booster. We'd like to do something quite funny. Could you—would you—ask that awfully clever P. G. Miss Harper to—help—no I don't mean exactly to help us. All we'd like is a suggestion from you two."

"We've heard about Miss Harper's wonderful stunts. We know what good shows you and Miss Page got up last year," interposed a tall girl with a frank, boyish face. "We were going to ask you and Miss Page when we passed, then we were afraid of interrupting your conversation."

"I wish you had," Marjorie said with smiling regret. "Miss Page is full of funny, original ideas. I'll speak to Miss Harper tonight. Why not come over to the Hall tomorrow evening? We can talk it over. Leila will have thought of some good stunt by then."

"Oh, fine, lovely, great work!" went up from her pleased listeners. "What time shall we come?" asked the little girl who reminded Marjorie of Susan Atwell, one of her Sanford schoolmates.

"Any time after seven, Miss Vernon," Marjorie said cordially.

The little girl showed pleased dimples at being thus remembered. The smiles of her companions were equally jubilant at the success of their plea. "Thank you, Miss Dean. We'll surely come," was Miss Vernon's grateful acceptance as the sextette took themselves off across the campus after a united murmur of thanks.

"The old calls are beginning to rise again," Marjorie reflected happily as she neared the Hall. She was reminded of the phrasing of the "Jungle Books," which she had adored as a child. "It's good hunting again on the campus. Good hunting all," she repeated half aloud, "good hunting all who keep the jungle laws."

CHAPTER XXII.
A "BOOSTER" PARADE

The "booster" parade for Augusta Forbes, candidate for sophomore presidency of at least half the sophomore class, was as ridiculous as its gleeful originators had intended it should be. Two evenings before the sophomore election the paraders issued from the gymnasium at dark, in amazing and flamboyant procession. A stolid drum major, Anna Perry was a triumph. She wore a scarlet cotton flannel uniform, recklessly trimmed in blue, and a high fur hat, contrived from an old squirrel muff. She led the van with a truly wonderful flourish of baton.

The presidential candidate came next in a two-wheeled push cart draped in red, white and blue bunting. Gussie, in an old black frock coat and trousers and a white plug hat which Leila had unearthed from among the Travelers stage properties was a figure of dignity in spite of the occasional sprawling lurch forward she gave in the cart. The cart was energetically motivated by four stalwart servitors. Their very energy made Gussie cling desperately to the rug-covered soap box on which she sat with one hand while she waved an acknowledgment with the other to the uproarious populace.

The vice president had also been selected for push cart honors. This dignitary's vehicle, however, while draped with equal gorgeousness was smaller and required only two lackeys. Richly attired in a pleated white shirt, fawn knickers, a blue plush smoking jacket and a black silk hat with a dent in one side of it, he sat flat in the bottom of the cart, recklessly distributing smiles and bows.

The treasurer and secretary came next in white flannel tennis trousers, white shoes and white silk blouses. They wore white sports hats wreathed in blue and scarlet, the sophomore colors. Unfortunately for them they had to be content with express wagons. As both candidates were tall they had to sit in their wagons, backs to the willing soph horses, a generous length of limb trailing over the rear end of their conveyances. It was either this, or a certain possibility of kicking their hard-working steeds. The rosy-faced manager of the Forbes' party rode in a child's dark blue automobile which she sturdily propelled with both feet, dressed in a plaided knicker suit, sneakers, a boy's striped sweater and a red and green monkey cap she looked not more than ten years old. Nor could a boy of that age have made more noise.

Behind her came the band, a ten-piece organization composed of one bugle, two accordions, two drums, one cornet, three combs and a hand organ. On each side of the procession walked the torch bearers lighting the impressive pageant with cat-tail torches. The dark-faced organ grinder in an old black velvet coat and blue overalls and fierce outstanding mustache closely resembled Calista Wilmot. He enthusiastically ground out a program of "Suwanee River," "Annie Laurie," "Get Out and Get Under," and "Do You Love Me, Honey?" while the rest of the band accompanied him with deafening zest.

Sauntering along behind this commotion and seemingly quite unruffled by it were no less than Uncle Sam, George Washington and Christopher Columbus. Their appearance on the campus was the signal for shrieks of mirth and they were hailed with the familiarity accorded to old friends. The parade circled Hamilton Hall three times then trailed down the main campus drive and rested there while the band gave an ear-splitting concert.

At the last the push cart detail tired of their hard but honored task and flatly refused to take the candidates a step further. The squabble ended by the squabblers walking off arm in arm toward the gymnasium where the sophs had made ready a spread of cake and ice cream to which anyone on the campus was welcome so long as the eats held out.

"It's almost safe to say that Gentleman Gus will be friend president," Jerry declared to Marjorie that night as the two were preparing for sleep. "I understand that she has over half the class with her."

"Oh, I think she'll win. I hope so." Marjorie became suddenly silent. "There are some of the sophs who still blame Gussie for what happened to Alma Hurst and Ida Weir," she said, after a little. "She was accused of having informed on two members of her class. She didn't, you know, and so do the rest of us. It was Miss Walbert who betrayed them."

"Why, old Marvelous Manager, what makes you so emphatic? Heard anything special about Gussie?" Jerry fixed interested eyes on Marjorie.

"Yes; today. Calista told me. Gussie doesn't know it. The other Bertram girls do. They won't tell her. She is so proud. They are afraid she'd withdraw from the nomination. They want her to be president because they think she'd make a fine one. Calista says the sophs are beginning to make a fuss over Miss Monroe. A freshie who lives at Acasia House began raving over Miss Monroe the first day she saw her. The very next day she sent her a big box of roses. The story went around the campus and the sophs heard it and began to rush Miss Monroe. She may be nominated at the class meeting Thursday."

"Maybe," Jerry conceded. "Still I think Gus has the inside track. The sophs may nominate half a dozen girls, but Gussie will carry off more than half the votes. You see if she doesn't. Don't worry about *her*."

"You are so cheering, Jeremiah. I did worry about Gussie, for her to hear anything horrid now, when she's so full of the election, would cut her to the heart.

"Cut it out, Bean, cut out worry, is the valuable advice of Dr. Macy. If you must worry, worry about me. I can't decide what I ought to study. I'm too highly educated now. My brain rebels against being stuffed any fuller. I'm what you might call wise in my own conceit."

"You're a cheerful goose," was Marjorie's fond opinion. Nevertheless she wished the eventful sophomore election were the next day instead of the day after.

CHAPTER XXIII.
STICKING IT OUT

"What is the news from the soph's election, I wonder? Ronny Lynde looked interestedly toward Hamilton Hall where the sophomore class had collected in a deserted recitation room to elect their officers.

"Here comes Muriel. Maybe she has heard echoes of the tumult that writhes within. What are *you* doing in the sacred corridors of Hamilton Hall?" Marjorie banteringly hailed. "You don't belong there." Marjorie and Ronny were passing Hamilton Hall on their way from a recitation in French Prose.

"Mayn't a mouse peep into a castle?" demanded Muriel. "I happen to be studying Greek, though I may not look it."

"Greek," Ronny meditatively repeated. "That might account for some of your strange actions. Things inexplicable are often remarked as being 'so much Greek.' I must say——"

"Don't say it," pleaded Muriel. Let me talk. The sophs are making a grand splatter and clatter at their meeting. It sounded almost as though they were engaged in mortal combat.

"I'd love to linger here and get the first news," Marjorie said with a bright glance into the open doorway of Hamilton Hall. "It's against P. G. dignity, though. Besides Professor Leonard wishes to see me at four-thirty in the gym. It's four-twenty-five now." She consulted her wrist watch. "I'll leave you two. Of course, if you should decide to wait for the election returns, it wouldn't be my fault," she told the two significantly.

"Such consideration for your friends," Muriel called after her. Marjorie made a derisive little gesture over one shoulder then quickened her step so as not to keep Professor Leonard waiting.

She found him in his office, his desk littered with physical culture programs which he was in process of making.

"So glad to see you, Miss Dean." He rose and offered her a friendly hand. "Sit down, and let us have one of our old-time inspiriting talks. I was hoping you would come back to the campus. I supposed you would be in Hamilton, at any rate. I wish you would tell me more about the new dormitory. I had no opportunity to talk with you about it last June."

Marjorie had intended to remain in the professor's office not more than a few moments. It was more nearly an hour before she rose to say good afternoon. Professor Leonard had strongly urged her to serve again on the sports committee. The energetic instructor had refused to entertain her doubt that the students of the college might prefer the sports committee should be seniors rather than post graduates.

"I can assure you of your eligibility to the committee," he said earnestly. "Yourself and two seniors, Miss Severn and Miss Moore, we will say, will make my perfect sports committee. However, think the matter over. I wish you to be satisfied. I know you are a very busy young woman. Help me, if you can. I need your judgment and support."

Marjorie reveled in the comforting inner assurance of work well done as she left the gymnasium and hastened toward Wayland Hall. She had decided before she reached the steps of the Hall, if Phil and Barbara wished very much that she should accept the honor the Professor had offered her, she would do so.

Glancing up at the chimes clock she saw a quarter to six staring her in the face. "Election's over long ago," she said to herself. "I'll have just about ten minutes to drop in on Gussie before dinner." "Oh, bother," was her second thought. "Gussie is probably out somewhere being rushed. I'll stop at her door, anyway." She hurried into the hall and made a running ascent of the stairs. She rapped repeatedly on Gussie's door; at first lightly, then with force. Still no one answered.

Going on to her own room she found the door half open and no Jerry in sight. She flung off her hat and long coat and set off for Ronny's room. The murmur of voices behind the closed door informed her that there someone was at home.

"Gadding again!" exclaimed Jerry as Marjorie walked into the room.

"I know you are, Jeremiah," Marjorie retorted sweetly. "It's surprising in you to own to it."

"I wasn't speaking of myself. Walking diagonally across the hall from one room to another isn't gadding. But you—That's another story."

"What about the election?" Marjorie made a scornful face at Jerry and turned to Ronny and Muriel. There was excitement in her question. She felt the same anxiety for Gussie that she would have for one of her chums in the same circumstances.

"Gentleman Gus was elected, but there was some sort of fuss," Muriel replied to the question. "We hung about the steps where we were when you left us. A crowd of sophs came out. Miss Monroe was with them. She was looking quite pleased with herself. She didn't see me. I mean she pretended she didn't. The other sophs, there were nine or ten of them, were peeved as could be. They were grumbling and muttering like a mob in a house play."

"Those sophs had undoubtedly backed Miss Monroe. We knew then she'd lost without having to be told, Muriel was anxious to find out the details so we went into Hamilton Hall to lie in wait for and pounce down upon someone who knew what we didn't," supplemented Ronny.

"By then we'd lost all respect for ourselves as P. G.'s," chuckled Muriel. "We were getting curiouser and curiouser. We did a wary toddle down the corridor toward the room the sophs were in. The door opened and out came Jane Everest. I can't recall when I've so much enjoyed meeting anyone," she declared waggishly. "Only Jane didn't know what the fuss was about. It was a hot one, she said between Gussie and some of the sophs we'd seen coming out of the Hall. Only the chairman and the election committee appeared to know what it was over."

"I'm afraid I know what it was over," Marjorie spoke with a kind of sad soberness. "You remember what I told you, Jeremiah?"

"Yes. I'm afraid you knew too much, Bean; too much." Jerry wagged her head with the air of a wiseacre.

Marjorie had to laugh in spite of her perturbation. Ronny and Muriel were eyeing her expectantly, listening for what she might say next.

"It is because of last year—" Marjorie broke off abruptly as a quick, imperative knock sounded at the door.

Ronny went to the door and opened it. "Oh, Gussie!" she exclaimed. "Come in."

"No, thank you. I—I—want to see—just Marjorie—no one else." Gussie's voice had a husky sound. Her eyelids were suspiciously pink.

"Why, Gussie!" Marjorie who had heard; was at the door with outstretched hands. "What is it, dear?" she asked in a lower tone.

"I must talk with you. A lot of miserable things have happened. I was elected. I don't want to be president. I don't know what to do." Gussie leaned her arm against a side of the open door, dropped her head upon it and burst into tears.

Next moment Marjorie had gently drawn the weeping sophomore inside the room and closed the door. "Poor old Gus," she soothed, "wrapping her arms about Augusta. Go ahead and cry as much as you please. You'll feel better afterward."

The three other girls now joined Marjorie in her earnest effort to comfort Augusta. In place of the breezy, self-reliant Gussie they had been used to meeting had now appeared this woe-begone, tear-drenched stranger.

"Buck up, Gentleman Gus," encouraged Jerry, giving the weeper a friendly slap between the shoulders.

The slangy consolation and the slap had a potent effect on Gussie. She stopped crying with a gulping sigh and even managed to coax a wavering, quivery smile to her lips.

"Ah, aha! That's better." Jerry made capital of the smile. "Have a chair, and tell us your troubles. If you see a chair here you fancy, grab it before anyone else has a chance at it. This isn't my room but I run it just the same. I run everything I can, and sometimes I get the run."

Gussie's smile grew at Jerry's nonsense. "No, I won't sit down. I can't stay. I ran away from the girls. I was looking for Marjorie." She stopped, looking distressed. "I'll tell you about the election," she slowly continued. "I wasn't going to tell anyone but Marjorie, but I'd like you to know." Her gaze swept the trio of girls. Apparently satisfied with what she saw, she said:

"There were three nominations for president—Miss Monroe, Evelyn Burtis and myself. The girls who were rooting for Miss Monroe were the ones who said I reported Ida Weir and Alma Hurst for hazing Flossie and me last year. You know I did not report Miss Weir and Miss Hurst. It was Miss Walbert who did that. I didn't know any such hateful thing had been said about me until Flossie told me after the election. If I had known it beforehand I wouldn't have accepted a nomination. Flossie knew it, and didn't tell me."

"Finally the voting began. I won by a third majority." Gussie could not keep a note of pride out of her voice. "Miss Monroe had more votes than Miss Burtis. My party began cheering me. Before they had stopped a soph who has a crush on Miss Monroe stood up and began fussing with the chairman. She said she had a perfect right to protest against the election; that the chairman had no business to accept my nomination for president when she had been informed beforehand by letter of my true character. She said that I was not fit to be the president of my class; that I was not truthful or honorable; that I had reported two worthy students for hazing who were entirely innocent of such a charge. Then she demanded that the ballot should be cast all over again with my name left out."

"The chairman said she had received the letter against me which the soph had written and had showed it to the other members of the committee. I wish you might have seen how scornful she looked. They had all agreed to ignore it as unworthy of attention."

"That chairman is a peach," warmly praised Jerry. "Who is she? I shall lunch her at Baretti's tomorrow. See if I don't."

"She is Miss Hopkins, and she is splendid." Gussie drew a long breath. "The soph who made all the fuss is Miss Walker. She and a pal of hers, Miss Johnson, were chummy with Alma Hurst and Ida Weir."

"It isn't right that such untruthful gossip should be spread about you, Gussie," was Marjorie's indignant cry. "The best way to down it is to show the sophs what a fine president you can be. I know you will."

"I—I said I would resign," Gussie confessed. "Miss Hopkins said she didn't blame me. She gave me a queer look when she said it as though she wished I wouldn't. My party hadn't heard much of the talk between Miss Walker and Miss Hopkins for Miss Walker was sitting on a front seat. They only knew it was some kind of kick about me. They began to cheer me and the other sophs began to hiss. My party raked them down. I was sitting near the front, too, with Floss and Calista. All of a sudden Miss Hopkins walked up to me and said: 'Please don't resign, Miss Forbes. The committee believe in you. I know you'll stand by us.' I couldn't resign after that." Gussie avowed with rueful emphasis.

"Your a real gentleman of the old school," Ronny approved. "Allow me to escort you to a blow-out at Baretti's. There is no time like the present. I'm going to gather in the Bertramites. Muriel, go gather in Leila and Vera. Tear them from the dining room table, if necessary."

"Slave, do my bidding," mocked Muriel as she bounced obediently from the room.

Veronica skipped lightly after her. She found the four Bertramites in Gussie's room, solemnly wondering where poor old Gus had hidden herself. Two minutes' explanation and the four girls were crossing the hall to Ronny's room, a hurrying quartette.

Muriel luckily caught Leila and Vera just outside the dining room.

"I know of no one more accommodating than myself, except Midget," was Leila's characteristic acceptance of the invitation. "Are we not noble to wait another hour for dinner when we are starving?"

"Noble isn't the word," Muriel returned effusively.

"You're too effusive to be sincere," was Vera's blunt opinion as the three started upstairs together.

Marjorie also had a good-will errand of her own to go on. Down stairs she quietly flitted and to the telephone. When she had finished a low-toned conversation with Robin Page at the other end of the line she hung up the receiver, clapped her hands childishly and ran upstairs, a demure little smile playing upon her lips.

Following Augusta Forbes' bitter cup of the afternoon the "blow-out" given in her honor by P. G.'s at Baretti's was an unexpected and effectual balm to her wounded spirit. It was a very jolly dinner, made thus by the handful of democratic girls who had "been through the Wars of the Campus," as Jerry announced in proposing a toast to the new sophomore president. Nor had their prompt upholding of Augusta been without effect on the several groups of girls who were also dining at the restaurant. At the Colonial the sophomore ringleaders in the ignoble attempt to down Gussie were dining Doris Monroe and hotly discussing ways and means by which their faction might gain the upper hand in sophomore affairs despite the loss of the presidency on the part of their choice.

Doris, in an exquisite frock of orchid tissue with a huge bunch of real pinky-lavender orchids trailing across one bare shoulder looked more like a fairy-tale princess than ever. Some of the sophs had even begun to call her the Princess. Nor could she know that Marjorie's flattering fancy of her, repeated to one of the Wayland Hall freshman by way of admiring Doris's undeniable beauty, was the source of the pleasing title. What Doris did know was that she had begun to crave popularity. She was having her first taste of the sweeping impetuous admiration of the American college girl. Under an air of sweetly-smiling but still indifferent amiability Doris was reaching greedily out for popularity. It would not be her fault if she should not gain it.

The crowning bliss of having faithful friends came to Gussie that night after she and her genial adherents had returned to Wayland Hall and she was in her room telling the details of the afternoon's fray to her curious chums. Under her window, sudden and sweet, the stately Hymn to Hamilton rose, more beautiful than ever by reason of the utter harmony of musical instruments and voices.

With one accord the five girls rushed to the two windows and opened them. Not one word did they speak, simply leaned across the sill and listened. When the hymn ended they applauded softly. The singers in the darkness below followed the hymn with one of Nevin's songs without words, vocalizing it perfectly. Then came "Appear Love At Thy Window," and last, "Good Night: God Guard You."

As the final line of the tender old song ended Gussie leaned far out the window and said in quiet, purposeful tones: "Thank you, everyone. You can't know how much you've done for me. I'll try harder than ever to live up to my Alma Mater."

From other windows on that side of the house girls were leaning, hurried to them by the harmonic sounds. In the room occupied by Muriel and the "Ice Queen" Doris Monroe had just entered. She was occupied in placing the bunch of orchids in water when the music began.

"What is it?" she languidly inquired as Muriel raced to a window and raised it.

"Serenade party. They are serenading Miss Forbes." Muriel's eyes danced as she gave the information.

"How peculiar!" drawled Doris. A jealous light had sprung into her changeable eyes.

"Not half so peculiar as the way some of the sophs behaved this afternoon." Muriel was constrained to retort over one shoulder as she dropped to her knees before the window.

CHAPTER XXIV.
A NEW ALLY

From the moment Doris Monroe had realized that she might become a figure of importance on the campus her attitude toward college had changed. In the summer she had scornfully regarded the campus as a "ghastly old space." Since the return to it of scores of smart, butterfly girls who owned cars and who made amusement a business during their recreation hours she had entirely altered her opinion.

Because she had chosen to be "miffed" at the Travelers during their summer stay at the Hall she still clung stubbornly to her groundless grudge against them. Then, too, Leslie Cairns had warned her against them. Leslie was a person for whom Doris had a certain amount of respect. Leslie had wealth in her own right and appeared to be afraid of no one. She had taken Doris for several rides in the white roadster and lunched and dined her expensively at exclusive wayside inns and tea rooms. When Leslie had returned to New York, shortly after Marjorie had returned to Sanford, Doris had missed her new acquaintance.

She was pleasantly surprised during the week following the sophomore election to find a note in the Hall bulletin board from Leslie Cairns. It read:

"Dear Doris:

"Meet me at the same old spot on the pike below the dago's tomorrow afternoon at five-thirty sharp. Hope you are well and enjoying the knowledge shop.

"Yours,

"Leslie."

"How are you?" was Leslie's nonchalant greeting of the sophomore when Doris arrived in the gathering October dusk at the rendezvous. She leaned out of the small black car she was driving and extended a careless hand to Doris. "Hop in," she invited. "We're off to Breton Hill for dinner. I'm going to zip this road wagon along when I clear Hamilton Estates."

"I'm so glad to see you again, Leslie," Doris said with more warmth than she usually exhibited.

"So you've come to life." Leslie grinned to herself as she started the car. "I had an idea you would. What's new at the knowledge shop?" There was a veiled eagerness in her question. Leslie cared far more about what went on at Hamilton than she pretended. "Tell me anything and everything you can think of."

"Things have livened immensely. I passed my soph exams and I was nominated for the soph presidency." Doris went on with a somewhat lofty account of the sophomore election and her sudden rise in campus popularity. "You ought to see the way the girls stare at me when I am out on the campus," she declared with enthusiasm. "I have some freshie crushes as well as sophs and some of the juniors and seniors are sweet to me. It's because I'm so beautiful," she added with cool assurance.

"Yes, you are a beauty," Leslie admitted half enviously. "Do you think you have half the college going?"

"Mercy no!" Doris truthfully exclaimed. "I might have, I think, if I could afford to entertain in a very exclusive expensive way. That's what counts. I have plenty of lovely clothes, but my father doesn't believe in giving me a large allowance. He would be awfully angry if he knew that I took half a room instead of the single he applied for for me. I did it so as to have that much more spending money. I wish now I hadn't. My roommate is Miss Harding, one of those horrid Sanford P. G.'s. She is snippy and so cheeky. A lot of the sophs are down on her and her crowd for boosting that stupid Miss Forbes for president."

"That was a favorite trick of Bean and her Beanstalks when I was at Hamilton," informed Leslie. She was regarding Doris's pretty discontented features as though revolving some plan in the dark recesses of her scheming mind.

"It seems to be a favorite trick still," replied Doris venomously. "I understand that Bean, as you call her, is trying to run the sports committee, take sides with one half the sophs and lecture the other half as to what they should do. She and that Miss Harper planned the election parade for Miss Forbes' crowd. I heard that the sophs who were trying to boost me asked her to help them get up a parade and she refused to help them."

"You sophs are foolish to stand such treatment." Leslie busied herself with the wheel as though offering casual opinion.

"What can we do?" demanded Doris fiercely. "It's hardly my place to start a fuss. I have a certain reputation as a beauty to keep up on the campus."

"Yes, that's so. You're clever enough to see it. Let me see." Leslie wrinkled her rugged features in intense concentration of thought. She was very desirous of hatching a plan of malicious action. It could hardly be traced to her, if carried out, she was reflecting comfortably.

"What the sophs should do is this," she said at length. "They should write two letters; both to Bean. One should be from the sophs themselves, calling Bean down for interfering with their interests and ordering her thereafter to mind her own affairs. The other—" Leslie hesitated. She wondered how much "Monroe would stand for." She continued, "The other should be from the seniors with a more polite intimation that they are capable of managing college sports without P. G. help."

"Oh, such letters couldn't be sent," vigorously disagreed Doris. "I wouldn't dare suggest any such thing to my soph crushes. As for the seniors—that would be hopeless!"

"All right. Forget it, and listen to me," Leslie ordered rather gruffly. "There's one thing I can do for you to help you with the popularity business. I'm going to lend you my white roadster. I haven't used it since I was here in the summer. It's in a Hamilton garage now. I'll pay for the up-keep of it a year in advance and run it up to the nearest garage to the campus. My garage will be ready by next spring, I hope. I'll blow you to a stunning white sports coat and other togs to match the 'Dazzler.' I'll open an account for you at the Hamilton Trust Company so you can entertain. I'll—"

"But, why—why should you do all this for me?" Doris cried wonderingly, stirred out of her usual high self-complacency. "I couldn't really accept so much from you, Leslie. You see—" her tones betrayed her reluctance to refuse Leslie's magnificently generous offer.

"Because I chose to do it. What's money to me? I'll help you make yourself the campus beauty and bring back the good old days on the campus when money counted for something. Bean and that set of mush heads have turned Hamilton into a regular goody-goody shop. The sophs who rooted for you have the right idea. I'm going to be around here all winter so I can tell you a few tricks you'll need to know."

"Oh, I don't know. I don't know," Doris repeated, as Leslie continued to put forward her offer. "My father has always said for me never to incur obligations. There's nothing I could do for you in return, Leslie, that would count for anything like what you'd be doing for me." She sighed enviously as she pictured herself in the white car.

"Yes, there are certain things you can do for me, later, when you've secured your own position on the campus." Leslie had been driving slowly as she talked. Now she stopped the car at the side of the road. "You can help me make matters uncomfortable for Bean and her crowd. You can—"

"I'm willing to do what I can, in my own way," Doris responded with a zest which betrayed her own rancor. "You can see for yourself, though, Leslie, that I couldn't do a thing such as you proposed about those letters."

Leslie laughed, silently, grotesquely. Doris could surely be trusted to look out for her own interests. "I said 'forget it' didn't I?" she reminded. Her tones, however, contained no mirth. She was inwardly scornful of Doris for her selfishness. Leslie had not the least intention of "forgetting," though Doris might.

CHAPTER XXV.
"ONLY SHADOWS"

"Three letters. That's not so bad." Marjorie triumphantly waved the trio of coveted envelopes about her head as she entered her room from a long interesting bout with chemistry. "I'm tired enough to enjoy my mail. Vera and I have been experimenting with a compound this whole afternoon. It should have come out black and it didn't—it came out a beautiful shade of green." Marjorie threw herself into a chair, laughing, and began picking open an envelope.

"The way of all great experimenters is hard," comforted Jerry. "Where's my mail? I didn't hear you say a word about it."

"Sorry to tell you, but there was none for you, Jeremiah."

"Your voice sounds sorrowful," Jerry returned with sarcasm. "Have some candy. I try always to be kind to those who are kind to me."

"I've heard you say so before." Marjorie was now spreading open the contents of the envelope she had torn across. She glanced at the letter. "Why-eee!" she exclaimed in a strained, unbelieving voice. She went on with a hurried perusal of the letter, then backed into a chair. "Listen to this, Jerry," she cried out in hurt tones:

"My Dear Miss Dean:

"While it is hard for me to put into words that which I have been asked to tell you I will try to do so as courteously as is possible in the circumstances. I have been chosen by the sophomore class with the exception of a few sophomores, to point out to you that your interference in class matters has created very bad feeling among the sophomores who believe themselves capable of adjusting any differences which may have arisen in the class.

"It is unfortunate that a post graduate of Hamilton College should be guilty of deliberate favoritism. You showed favoritism to Miss Forbes before and have done so since the sophomore election. Miss Forbes received the nomination for the presidency as a result of your "boosting." Many of the sophomores who voted for her because of a high, but misplaced respect for you, now know their mistake. Miss Forbes deserved the censure she received at the election. The manner in which you and other post-graduates babied her afterward I now venture to criticize.

"The sophomore class are of an almost united opinion that they may be trusted to carry on their business wisely and with justice to all. I am confident that, released from any responsibility you may have taken upon yourself regarding them, you will have more time to pursue your own important affairs.

"Sincerely,

"LOUISE MAY WALKER."

"Don't let a little thing like that bother you," Jerry's eyes shone with sympathy in spite of her sturdily careless tone. "A girl who would write such a letter isn't worth minding. Don't let it mislead you. The sophs' united opinion is probably about ten or twelve strong, and not more. Keep right on going, Bean. You shouldn't worry." Jerry's cheerful smile broke broadly out like the sun from behind a cloud.

Marjorie, looking up from a second reading of the letter, returned the smile ruefully. "I care," she said reflectively, "and I don't care. I thought I was awfully hurt, but I'm up and on my feet now, brushing off the dust. I wouldn't have done things differently about Gussie. I suppose favoritism means helping get up the parade and Ronny's dinner to Gus at Baretti's. We would have helped the other soph faction with a parade just as quickly if they had come to us. I think I'll go on with my letters."

Marjorie tore open the second envelope with decision. A glance at its contends and she exclaimed in righteous indignation: "Why, the idea! This is too ridiculous for words!" She read aloud rapidly:

"Dear Miss Dean:

"We understand that Professor Leonard has asked you to serve again on the senior sports committee. Do you not agree with us that it would be more becoming in you to give place to a member of the senior class. We have been informed that such a decision on your part would be welcomed by the other members of the committee.

"Yours very truly,

"SENIOR WELFARE COMMITTEE."

"That's a fake," pronounced Jerry, instantly. "You know and so do I that Barbara Severn and Phil are glad as can be that you are going to serve on committee with them this year. Whoever wrote this bluff didn't know that. Any student who was here last year knows how chummy you were with both Phil and Barbara. Ha; great head!" Jerry whacked herself smartly on the top of the head. "How rough you are, Jeremiah!" She fell to rubbing her injured head. "I wish Hamilton offered a course in how to be a detective. I have the investigator's brain."

"Then take this case and find out who wrote this letter," Marjorie tossed the second letter into Jerry's lap. "I'm not going to answer Miss Walker's letter. It needs no reply." The sudden firm set of her lovely face showed the girl's underlying strong character. "Thank fortune," she said in relief, "*this* letter is from Miss Susanna. No hateful surprises this time. Her inflection grew unconsciously tender as she read to Jerry:

"Dear, Dear Child:

"There's a gala day ahead of us. Two weeks from Saturday afternoon we are to go to the dormitory site to assist in the laying of the cornerstone. Peter Graham says it will be ready to lay on that day, November sixth, at three o'clock in the afternoon. Bring the rest of the Travelers to tea on next Sunday evening and we will talk about the great occasion. I am notifying you of it thus long beforehand so that none of the Travelers will make any other engagements for that day. I shall expect you on Sunday afternoon.

"Affectionately,

"SUSANNE CRAIG HAMILTON."

Marjorie raised her head from the reading of this comforting letter, her whole face radiant with returned good cheer. "I feel all 'chirked' up again. Jeremiah." She patted the letter and laid it against her cheek. "The persons who wrote those other two letters are only the shadows; mean, skulking shadows that can't bear the light. Miss Susanna is the substance. That's why I love her so much."

"You're an April Bean," was Jerry's indulgent but irrelevant reply. "One minute you cloud over and the next you shine. Now listen to my ambitions. I'm going to shadow some of those skulking shadows you just mentioned and solve the riddle of who writ the wrote. The weary chase may lead me over land and sea, or, at least, all over the campus. Then Bean," Jerry raised a melodramatic hand above her head, "beloved Bean, your wrongs shall be avenged."

CHAPTER XXVI.
THE CORNERSTONE

Saturday, the sixth of November, found a buoyant band of Travelers taking the well worn road to the dormitory site. They had decided to walk rather than ride, having agreed that there would be an elation of spirit attending that happy march which the little journey, if made by automobile, could not furnish.

Whatever plans Miss Susanna had made for the auspicious occasion she had not divulged. She had talked with them freely enough concerning the laying of the cornerstone on the Sunday evening on which they had had tea at the Arms. She had playfully ordered her young friends each to think of some good wish they might offer in behalf of the dormitory. Each was then to put her wish on paper, seal the paper in an envelope and have it ready to cast into the hollowed space of the cornerstone itself.

The day before the ceremony Miss Susanna had sent a note to Jerry by Jonas requesting her to be at the Arms by two o'clock on the Saturday afternoon of the eventful day. Jerry had not the least idea of why she should suddenly have come into demand by the erratic old lady of the Arms. To hear Miss Susanna, or rather to hear from her, was to obey. Jerry marched off to the Arms dressed in a most "spiffy" fall suit of a new shade of blue that became her vastly.

At the dormitory where the confusion of demolishment had reigned so long, all was now in order, the order of progressive building. The ground above the vast cellar where the stone foundation would rise had been leveled, all debris had been cleared away and the great cornerstone placed ready for its descent into place.

Close to it a considerable number of workmen were gathered. Now in neat dark clothing instead of overalls. They had been invited by Miss Susanna to attend the ceremony and were to be given a luncheon at Hamilton Arms afterward. This was to be Jonas' treat. Standing with them, his dark face wreathed in smiles as he talked to Peter Graham was Signor Baretti. Next to the Travelers there was no one more enthusiastic over the dormitory than Baretti.

"Look at Mr. Graham," were Ronny's low-spoken words as she and Robin and Marjorie paused three abreast near the cornerstone. "He's perfectly happy. His face is so bright its positively dazzling."

"He has the conscientiousness of work well done," Robin returned in the same soft tone.

"That's precisely it, Robin," nodded Marjorie. "I've been watching him and trying to analyze his expression."

"Miss Susanna will be late for the cornerstone act if she doesn't appear in just four more minutes," remarked Muriel practically.

"My, what a reverent spirit of mind you are in," satirized Ronny. "'Cornerstone act!' I'm shocked."

"I hope you recover. Why here comes a car! That's not Miss Susanna's turn-out. No horses in sight, either." Muriel forgot to bicker with Ronny in her excitement over the rapidly approaching car.

As it came nearer the group of girls recognized a familiar figure on the front seat. It was Jerry, and she was driving. Beside her sat Jonas, his laughing features showing what he thought of the surprise.

"Jeremiah!" went up in a merry little shout from the Travelers.

"Yes, Jeremiah." Jerry smiled complacently on her chums then slid out of the car and opened one of the rear doors of the limousine as Jonas opened the other.

Out of the limousine on one side came the Reverend Compton Greene, of Hamilton Estates, the oldest minister in the county of Hamilton. From the other side emerged Professor Wenderblatt, President Matthews and, last of all, gallantly assisted by the president came Miss Susanna.

Instead of being impressed into silence by sight of distinguished Prexy the Travelers vented a shout which more than energetically expressed their sentiments.

"How do you like my new car, children?" briskly inquired Miss Hamilton, showing frank delight at the prank she had played on her girls. "And how do you like my driver? Well, I had to come to it. I mean about the automobile. Jonas will learn to drive the car. I sha'n't let him drive much faster than at a crawl. How are you, Peter?" She addressed her old friend with every mark of kindly affection.

"It's a happy day for me, Susanna," he said, his bright face faintly flushed and free from worry seemed that of a young man. Only the thick white hair brushed off his forehead proclaimed him to be in the winter of life. "And I have you to thank for it."

"Thank yourself, Peter; not me. 'The laborer is worthy of his hire.' Never forget that. Come, Dr. Greene," she turned to the old minister; "let me present my young campus friends to you. And here is Signor Baretti who is a loyal supporter of the dormitory cause."

The last of the Hamiltons introduced the Travelers, one by one to the old minister. She talked animatedly with one of her party, then another. "I felt that I ought not invite Professor Wenderblatt's daughter today without inviting her distinguished father," she laughingly told Lillian Wenderblatt. In a pale gray silk gown with a beautiful gray carriage coat lined in white and a gray lace hat trimmed with a cluster of pale silk violets, Miss Susanna appeared to have shed the stiff, repressed air that had formerly hung over her.

This thought sprang to Marjorie's mind as the old lady walked confidently about among the company and exchanged sociabilities with them. Marjorie looked up to find Jonas' eyes fixed earnestly upon her. He glanced significantly at Miss Susanna and back to her again. She understood that he wished her to know and share his pleasure at the happiness of "Mr. Brooke's little girl."

Presently the company strolled to a place near the corner where the great stone would soon be set in place. There was a brief prayer in behalf of those who had gathered there to view the result of their generous efforts. Then they all sang "Blessed Be the Tie That Binds," a favorite hymn of Brooke Hamilton's. Miss Susanna led in her clear old treble. There were speeches from the men, even one from Signor Baretti, who responded as nobly as his limited English would permit. Miss Susanna refused to make a speech, nor could Jonas be induced to make one. Neither did Page and Dean take kindly to speech-making.

President Matthew's earnest ringing address pleased Miss Susanna most of all. She made mental note that there was nothing mean-spirited about "that man, Matthews." Then the workmen, under Peter Graham's direction, came forward to place the stone and the girls and Miss Susanna dropped their envelopes into the hollowed opening. Professor Wenderblatt placed an old German writing, religious in character, with the other envelopes. The rest of the men dropped in gold and silver pieces.

As the huge block of stone was settled in the earthy pocket made for it the company joined hands and sang a verse of "Auld Lang Syne." Miss Susanna, tears running down her cheeks, shook hands with Peter Graham and then with Jonas. They represented her only friends for many years.

"I am going to tell you all," she said, wiping her eyes and then her glasses, "that this dear child here is responsible for anything I've lately done that Uncle Brooke would have wished done." She drew Marjorie, who stood beside her, into the curve of her arm. "I cannot carry out his wishes in the way I had once planned for the college. I am sorry. I never used to be sorry. I have grown graciousness, it would seem." She looked defiantly toward President Matthews.

"Hamilton College is grateful to you already for many favors," the president returned with a gentle courtesy that caused two bright color signals to flash into Miss Susanna's cheeks.

"I've thought something out," Marjorie remarked suddenly to Ronny when, a little later, the party of Travelers went their way toward the campus. "It's about Miss Susanna. I used to think, when first I knew her, that it would be splendid if she'd give the college material for Brooke Hamilton's biography, even if she didn't wish to give it. Now I know the gift without the giver would be bare. Nothing she might give the college that had been Mr. Brooke's would be worth anything without her approval."

"She will soften some day. Remember what I say," Ronny predicted. "Look how much she has done already for the college, through us, since we have known her. Did she tell you what she wrote and put in her envelope?"

"No, I forgot to ask her. What was it?"

"She wouldn't tell me. She said it would break the spell if she told and what she had wished might not come true. Of course she was joking, but she kept what she wrote a secret."

"We never thought on the night we came to Hamilton, lonely freshies, and went out hungrily to hunt dinner that we'd be building a dormitory not far from where we ate our first meal," Marjorie said musingly.

"What a stormy time we had that year! Now we may enjoy the peaceful pleasure of the P. G.," Ronny was lightly mocking.

Marjorie smiled to herself. Into her mind had come remembrance of the two disturbing letters she had lately received. Jerry's efforts to discover the author of the one had been fruitless. Marjorie had proudly ignored the writer of the other. Such letters did not argue well for the "peaceful pleasures of the P. G."

"Your days of peaceful P. G. pleasure are over, Veronica Browning Lynne. You may manage the first show we shall give."

"'Let us then be up and doing, with a heart for any fate,'" Ronny quoted, striking an attitude.

"Something like that." Marjorie caught Ronny's upraised arm and drew it under her own. Ronny had brought to mind the inspiring old poem she had so greatly loved and clung to in her grammar school days. Now as ever her soul answered the call of it.

How she made it her watchword through the rest of the college year amid many perplexities and vexations will be told in: "MARJORIE DEAN, MARVELOUS MANAGER."

Lightning Source UK Ltd.
Milton Keynes UK
UKHW010745271222
414464UK00004B/297